Roba

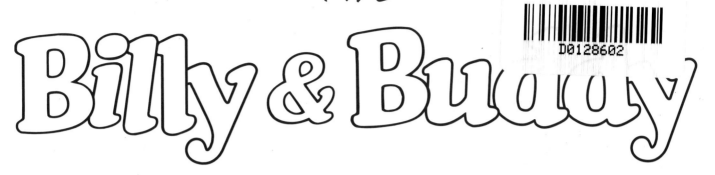

Billy & Buddy

BEWARE OF (FUNNY) DOG!

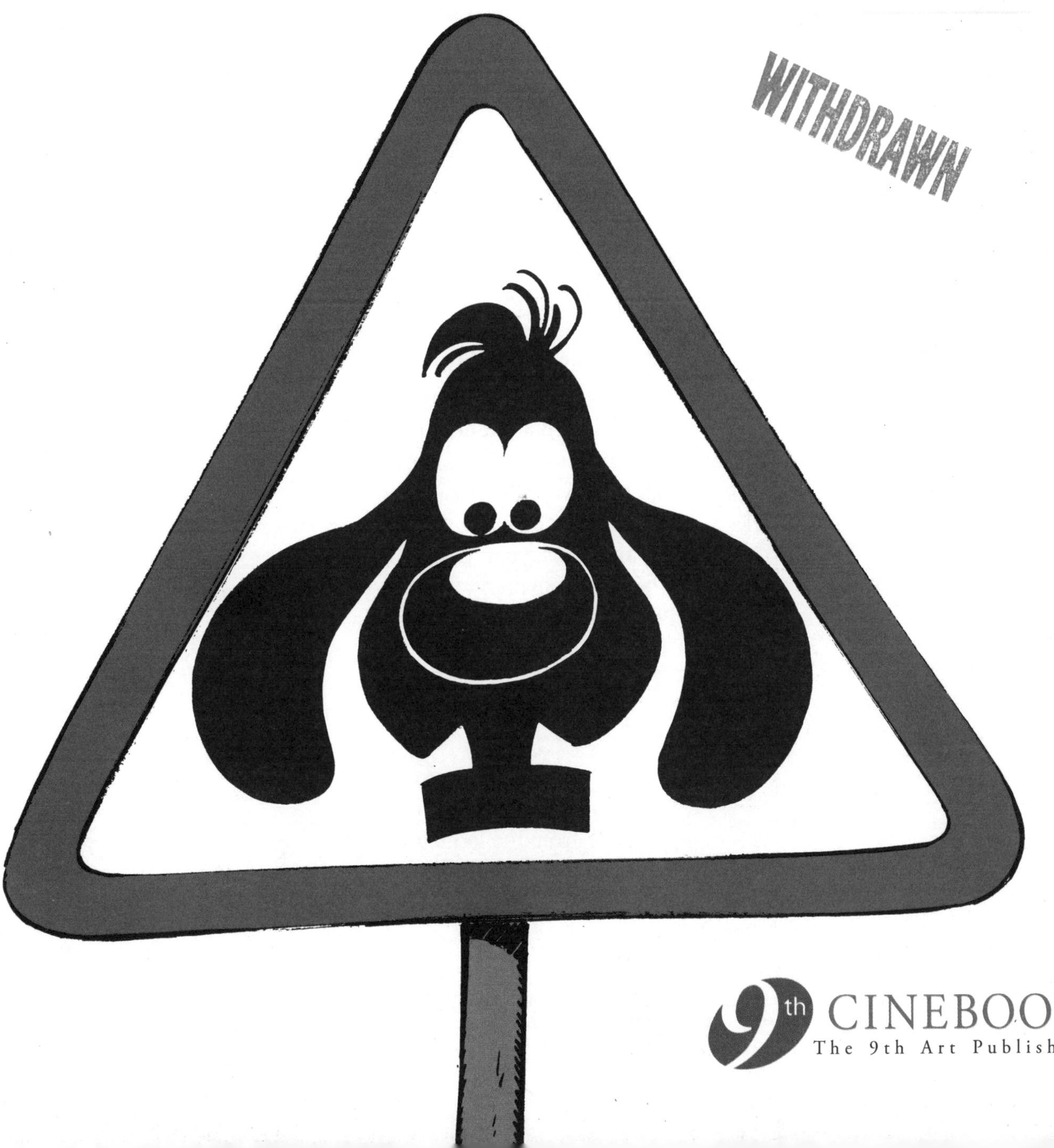

9th CINEBOOK
The 9th Art Publisher

Original title: Boule & Bill 15 – Attention chien marrant !
Original edition: © Dupuis, 1974 by Roba
© Studio Boule & Bill 2019
www.bouleetbill.com
All rights reserved
English translation: © 2019 Cinebook Ltd
Translator: Jerome Saincantin
Editor: Erica Olson Jeffrey
Lettering and text layout: Design Amorandi
Printed in Spain by EGEDSA
This edition first published in Great Britain in 2019 by
Cinebook Ltd
56 Beech Avenue
Canterbury, Kent
CT4 7TA
www.cinebook.com
A CIP catalogue record for this book
is available from the British Library
ISBN 978-1-84918-457-1

9th CINEBOOK
The 9th Art Publisher

Cleaned Out

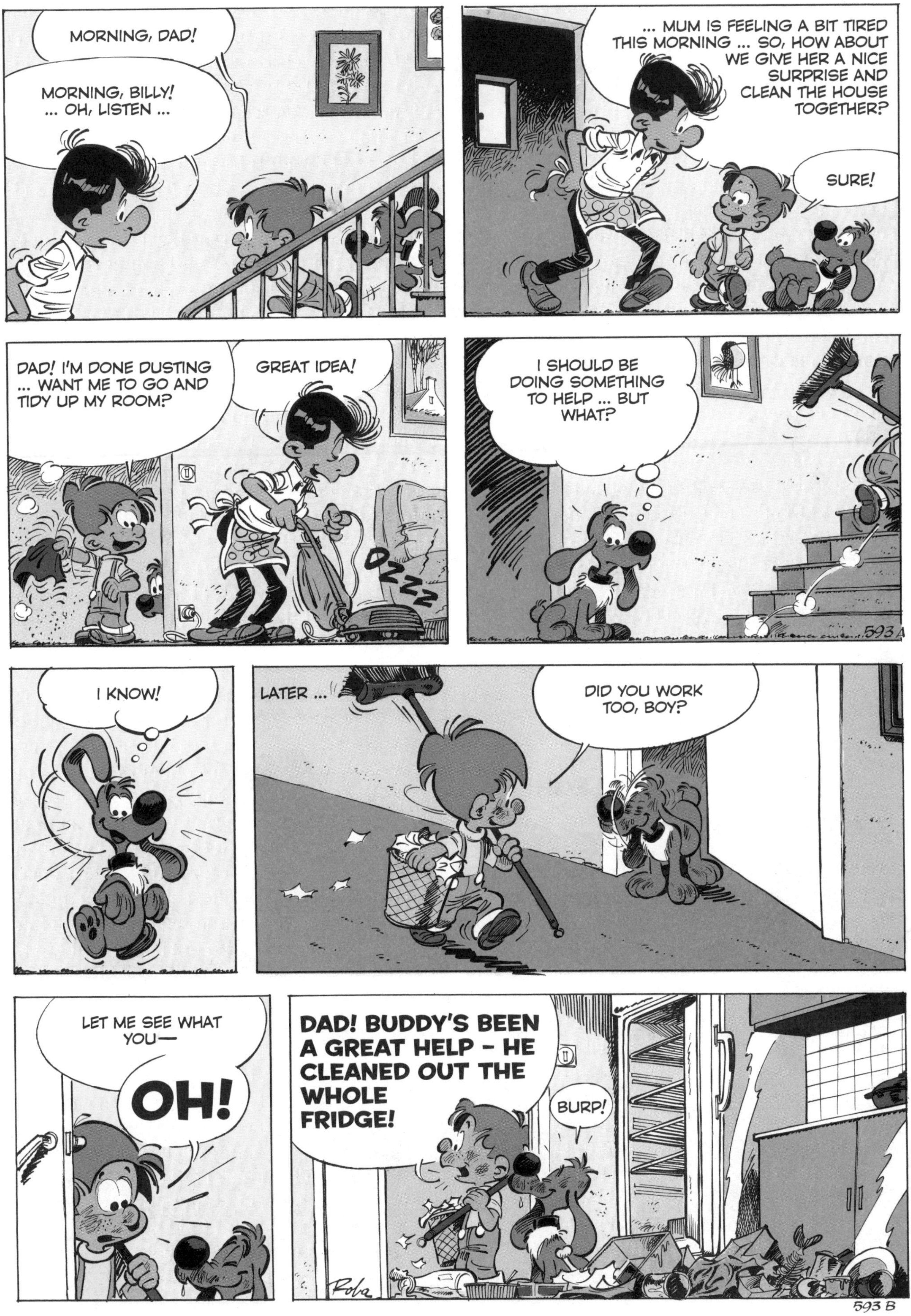

MORNING, DAD!
MORNING, BILLY! ... OH, LISTEN ...
... MUM IS FEELING A BIT TIRED THIS MORNING ... SO, HOW ABOUT WE GIVE HER A NICE SURPRISE AND CLEAN THE HOUSE TOGETHER?
SURE!
DAD! I'M DONE DUSTING ... WANT ME TO GO AND TIDY UP MY ROOM?
GREAT IDEA!
OZZZZ
I SHOULD BE DOING SOMETHING TO HELP ... BUT WHAT?
593 A
I KNOW!
LATER ...
DID YOU WORK TOO, BOY?
LET ME SEE WHAT YOU—
OH!
DAD! BUDDY'S BEEN A GREAT HELP - HE CLEANED OUT THE WHOLE FRIDGE!
BURP!
Roba
593 B

Bad Mood

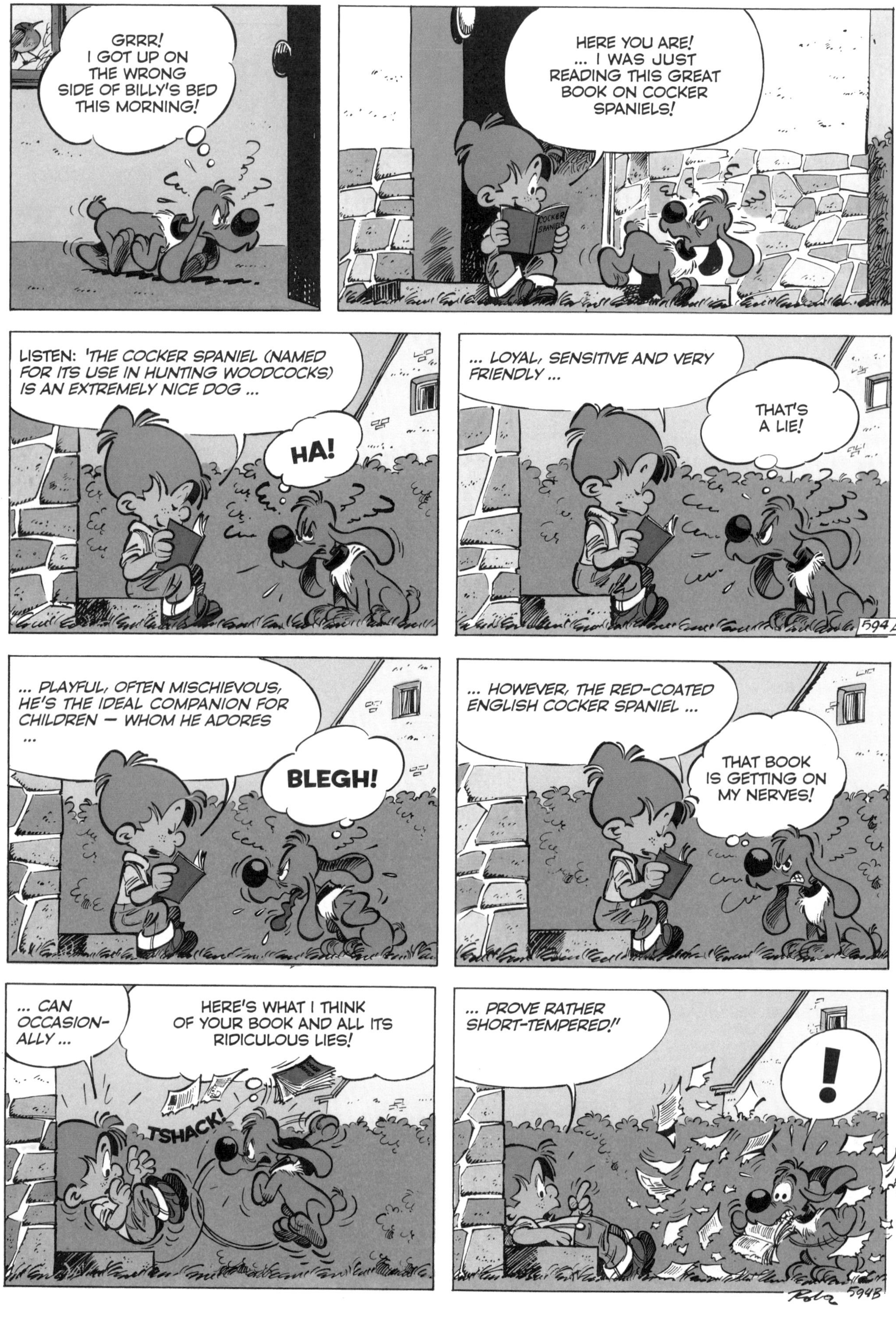

GRRR! I GOT UP ON THE WRONG SIDE OF BILLY'S BED THIS MORNING!
HERE YOU ARE! ... I WAS JUST READING THIS GREAT BOOK ON COCKER SPANIELS!
COCKER SPANIELS
LISTEN: 'THE COCKER SPANIEL (NAMED FOR ITS USE IN HUNTING WOODCOCKS) IS AN EXTREMELY NICE DOG ...
HA!
... LOYAL, SENSITIVE AND VERY FRIENDLY ...
THAT'S A LIE!
594 A
... PLAYFUL, OFTEN MISCHIEVOUS, HE'S THE IDEAL COMPANION FOR CHILDREN — WHOM HE ADORES ...
BLEGH!
... HOWEVER, THE RED-COATED ENGLISH COCKER SPANIEL ...
THAT BOOK IS GETTING ON MY NERVES!
... CAN OCCASION-ALLY ...
HERE'S WHAT I THINK OF YOUR BOOK AND ALL ITS RIDICULOUS LIES!
TSHACK!
... PROVE RATHER SHORT-TEMPERED!'
!
Roba
594B

Hey, Chaps!

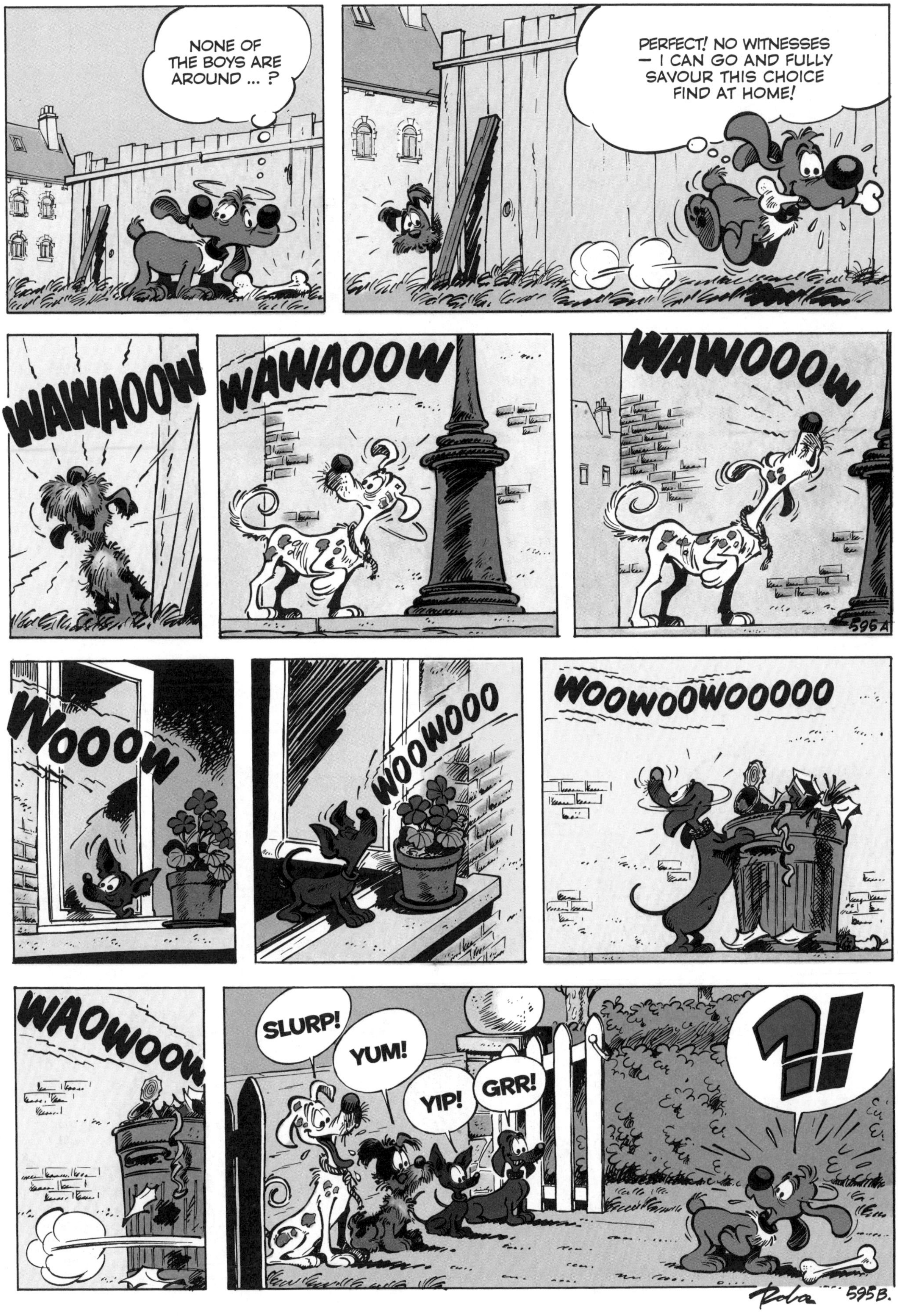
NONE OF THE BOYS ARE AROUND ... ?
PERFECT! NO WITNESSES — I CAN GO AND FULLY SAVOUR THIS CHOICE FIND AT HOME!
WAWAOOW
WAWAOOW
WAWOOOW
595 A
WOOOW
WOOWOOO
WOOWOOWOOOOO
WAOWOOW
SLURP!
YUM!
YIP!
GRR!
?!
Roba
595B.

Schoolyard Blues

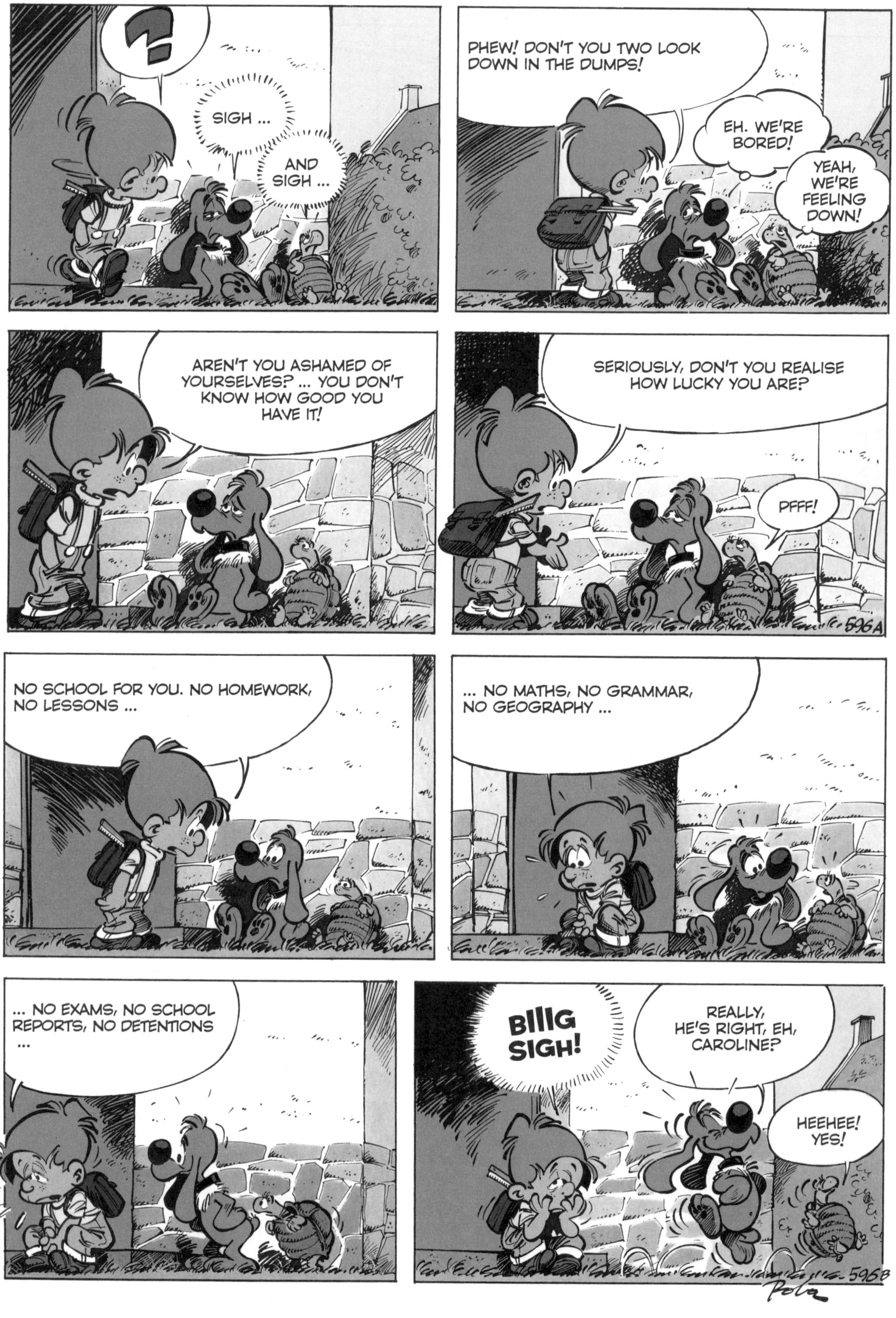

?
SIGH ...
AND SIGH ...
PHEW! DON'T YOU TWO LOOK DOWN IN THE DUMPS!
EH. WE'RE BORED!
YEAH, WE'RE FEELING DOWN!
AREN'T YOU ASHAMED OF YOURSELVES? ... YOU DON'T KNOW HOW GOOD YOU HAVE IT!
SERIOUSLY, DON'T YOU REALISE HOW LUCKY YOU ARE?
PFFF!
596A
NO SCHOOL FOR YOU. NO HOMEWORK, NO LESSONS ...
... NO MATHS, NO GRAMMAR, NO GEOGRAPHY ...
... NO EXAMS, NO SCHOOL REPORTS, NO DETENTIONS ...
BIIIG SIGH!
REALLY, HE'S RIGHT, EH, CAROLINE?
HEEHEE! YES!
596B

Auction Hero

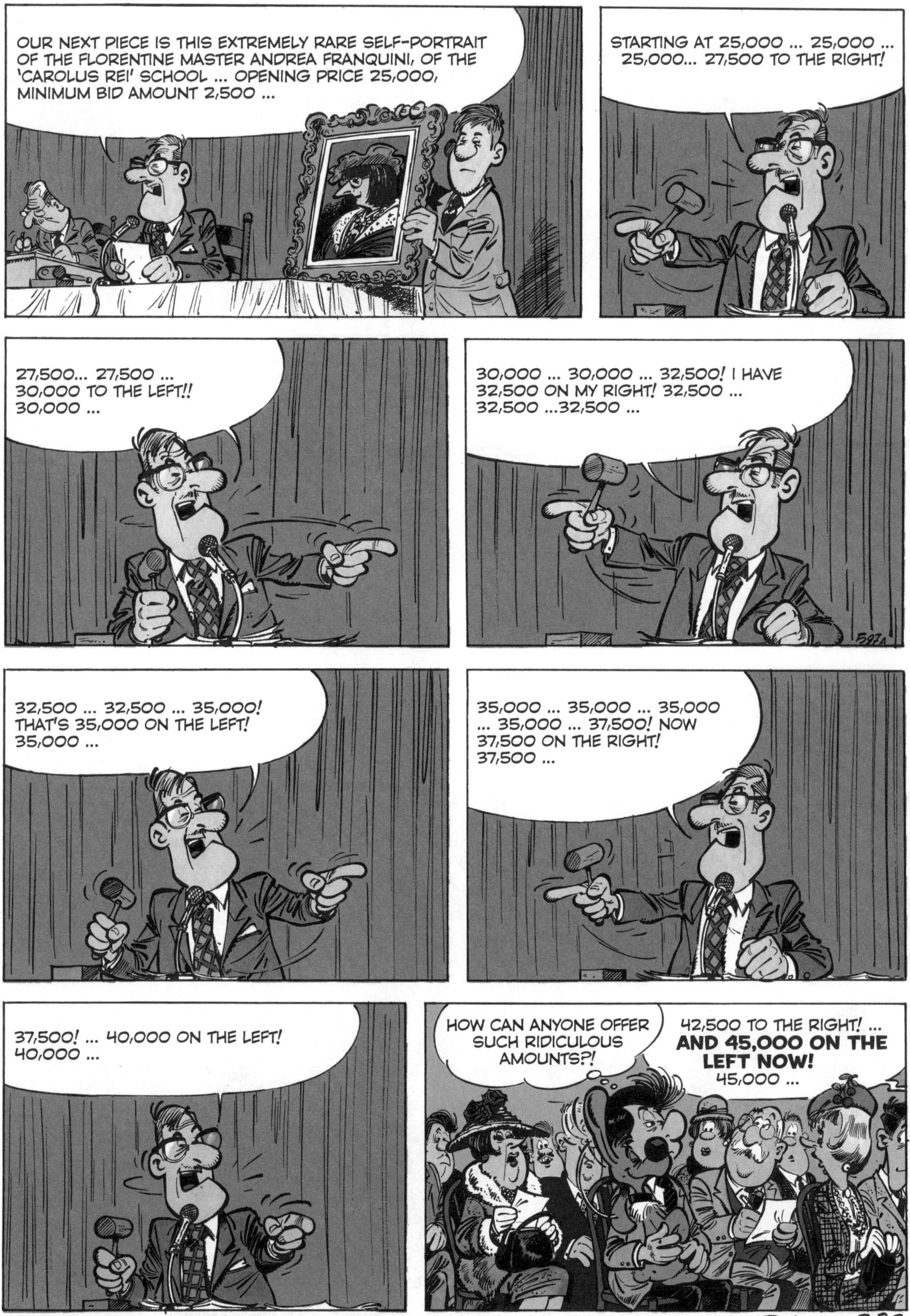
OUR NEXT PIECE IS THIS EXTREMELY RARE SELF-PORTRAIT OF THE FLORENTINE MASTER ANDREA FRANQUINI, OF THE 'CAROLUS REI' SCHOOL ... OPENING PRICE 25,000, MINIMUM BID AMOUNT 2,500 ...
STARTING AT 25,000 ... 25,000 ... 25,000... 27,500 TO THE RIGHT!
27,500... 27,500 ... 30,000 TO THE LEFT!! 30,000 ...
30,000 ... 30,000 ... 32,500! I HAVE 32,500 ON MY RIGHT! 32,500 ... 32,500 ...32,500 ...
32,500 ... 32,500 ... 35,000! THAT'S 35,000 ON THE LEFT! 35,000 ...
35,000 ... 35,000 ... 35,000 ... 35,000 ... 37,500! NOW 37,500 ON THE RIGHT! 37,500 ...
37,500! ... 40,000 ON THE LEFT! 40,000 ...
HOW CAN ANYONE OFFER SUCH RIDICULOUS AMOUNTS?!
42,500 TO THE RIGHT! ... **AND 45,000 ON THE LEFT NOW!** 45,000 ...
Rola 597B.

With Bells On

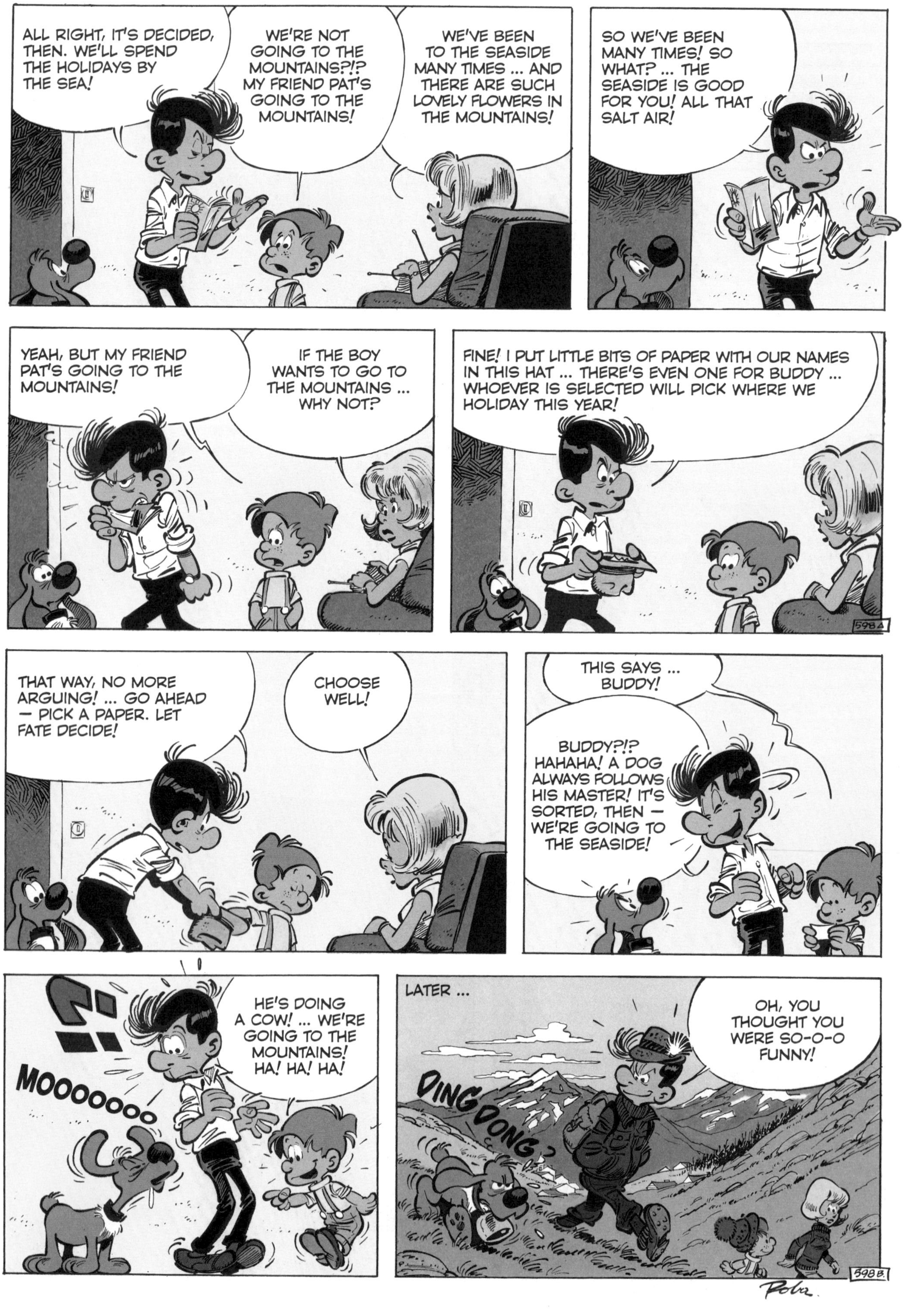

ALL RIGHT, IT'S DECIDED, THEN. WE'LL SPEND THE HOLIDAYS BY THE SEA!
WE'RE NOT GOING TO THE MOUNTAINS?!? MY FRIEND PAT'S GOING TO THE MOUNTAINS!
WE'VE BEEN TO THE SEASIDE MANY TIMES ... AND THERE ARE SUCH LOVELY FLOWERS IN THE MOUNTAINS!
SO WE'VE BEEN MANY TIMES! SO WHAT? ... THE SEASIDE IS GOOD FOR YOU! ALL THAT SALT AIR!
YEAH, BUT MY FRIEND PAT'S GOING TO THE MOUNTAINS!
IF THE BOY WANTS TO GO TO THE MOUNTAINS ... WHY NOT?
FINE! I PUT LITTLE BITS OF PAPER WITH OUR NAMES IN THIS HAT ... THERE'S EVEN ONE FOR BUDDY ... WHOEVER IS SELECTED WILL PICK WHERE WE HOLIDAY THIS YEAR!
598A
THAT WAY, NO MORE ARGUING! ... GO AHEAD — PICK A PAPER. LET FATE DECIDE!
CHOOSE WELL!
THIS SAYS ... BUDDY!
BUDDY?!? HAHAHA! A DOG ALWAYS FOLLOWS HIS MASTER! IT'S SORTED, THEN — WE'RE GOING TO THE SEASIDE!
MOOOOOOO
HE'S DOING A COW! ... WE'RE GOING TO THE MOUNTAINS! HA! HA! HA!
LATER ...
OH, YOU THOUGHT YOU WERE SO-O-O FUNNY!
DING DONG
598B
Roba

Mountain Dogs

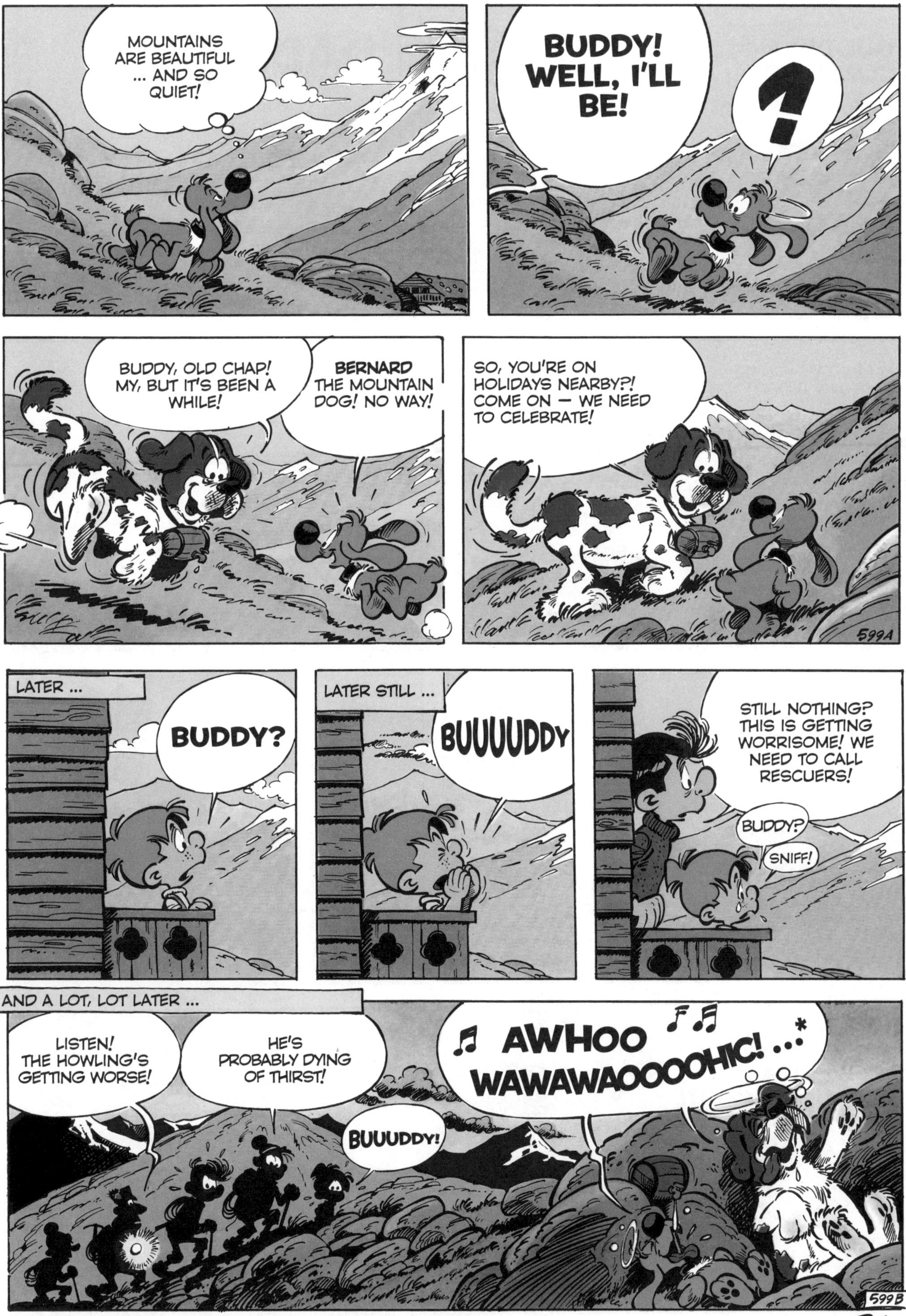

MOUNTAINS ARE BEAUTIFUL ... AND SO QUIET!
BUDDY! WELL, I'LL BE!
?
BUDDY, OLD CHAP! MY, BUT IT'S BEEN A WHILE!
BERNARD THE MOUNTAIN DOG! NO WAY!
SO, YOU'RE ON HOLIDAYS NEARBY?! COME ON — WE NEED TO CELEBRATE!
599A
LATER ...
BUDDY?
LATER STILL ...
BUUUUDDY
STILL NOTHING? THIS IS GETTING WORRISOME! WE NEED TO CALL RESCUERS!
BUDDY?
SNIFF!
AND A LOT, LOT LATER ...
LISTEN! THE HOWLING'S GETTING WORSE!
HE'S PROBABLY DYING OF THIRST!
BUUUDDY!
AWHOO WAWAWAOOOOHIC! ...*
599B

*SHE'LL BE COMING ROUND THE MOUNTAINHIC! ...

Peak Holidays

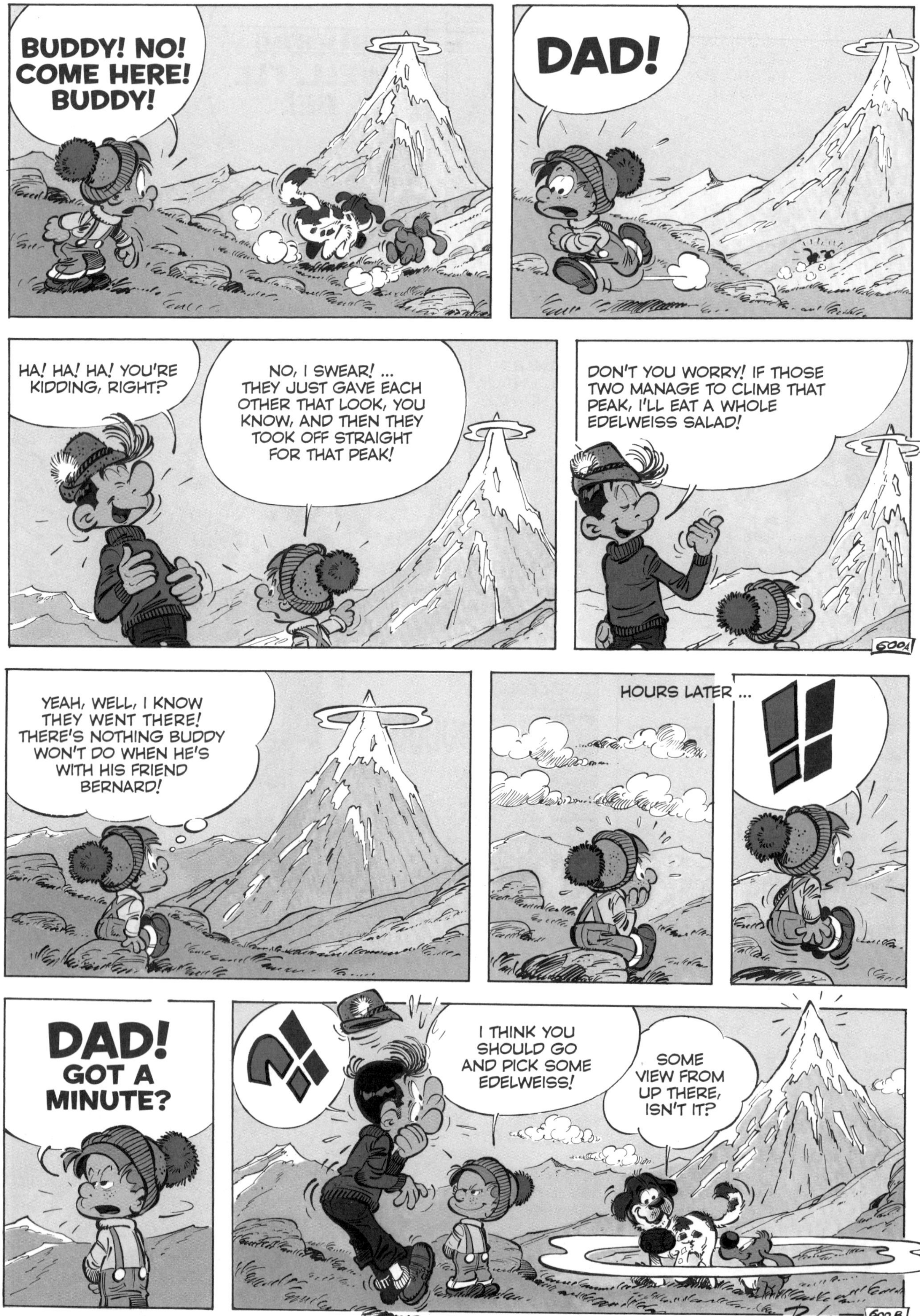

BUDDY! NO! COME HERE! BUDDY!
DAD!
HA! HA! HA! YOU'RE KIDDING, RIGHT?
NO, I SWEAR! ... THEY JUST GAVE EACH OTHER THAT LOOK, YOU KNOW, AND THEN THEY TOOK OFF STRAIGHT FOR THAT PEAK!
DON'T YOU WORRY! IF THOSE TWO MANAGE TO CLIMB THAT PEAK, I'LL EAT A WHOLE EDELWEISS SALAD!
YEAH, WELL, I KNOW THEY WENT THERE! THERE'S NOTHING BUDDY WON'T DO WHEN HE'S WITH HIS FRIEND BERNARD!
HOURS LATER ...
DAD! GOT A MINUTE?
I THINK YOU SHOULD GO AND PICK SOME EDELWEISS!
SOME VIEW FROM UP THERE, ISN'T IT?

Edelweiss

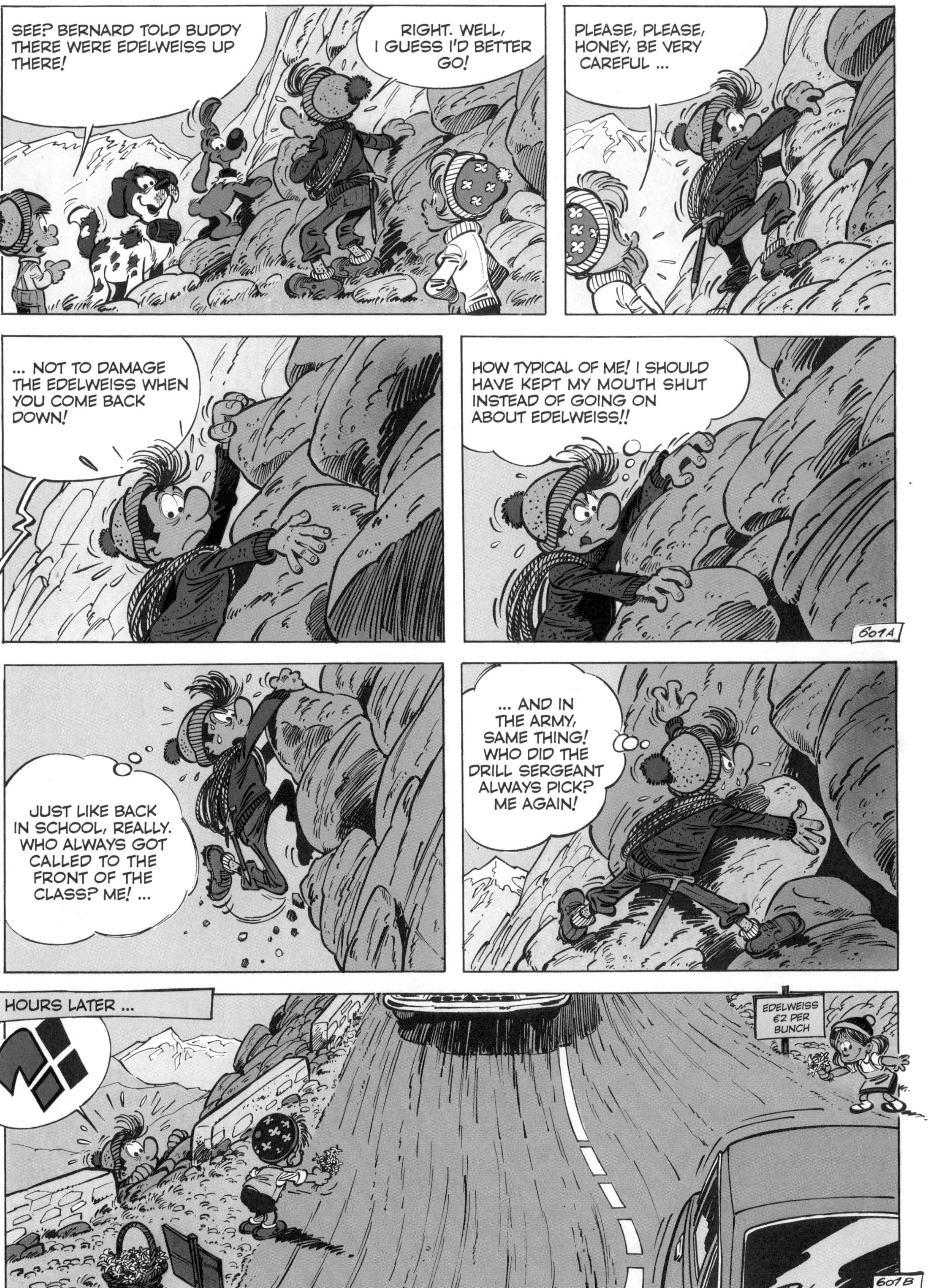

SEE? BERNARD TOLD BUDDY THERE WERE EDELWEISS UP THERE!
RIGHT. WELL, I GUESS I'D BETTER GO!
PLEASE, PLEASE, HONEY, BE VERY CAREFUL ...
... NOT TO DAMAGE THE EDELWEISS WHEN YOU COME BACK DOWN!
HOW TYPICAL OF ME! I SHOULD HAVE KEPT MY MOUTH SHUT INSTEAD OF GOING ON ABOUT EDELWEISS!!
601A
JUST LIKE BACK IN SCHOOL, REALLY. WHO ALWAYS GOT CALLED TO THE FRONT OF THE CLASS? ME! ...
... AND IN THE ARMY, SAME THING! WHO DID THE DRILL SERGEANT ALWAYS PICK? ME AGAIN!
HOURS LATER ...
EDELWEISS €2 PER BUNCH
601B

Do You Fondue?

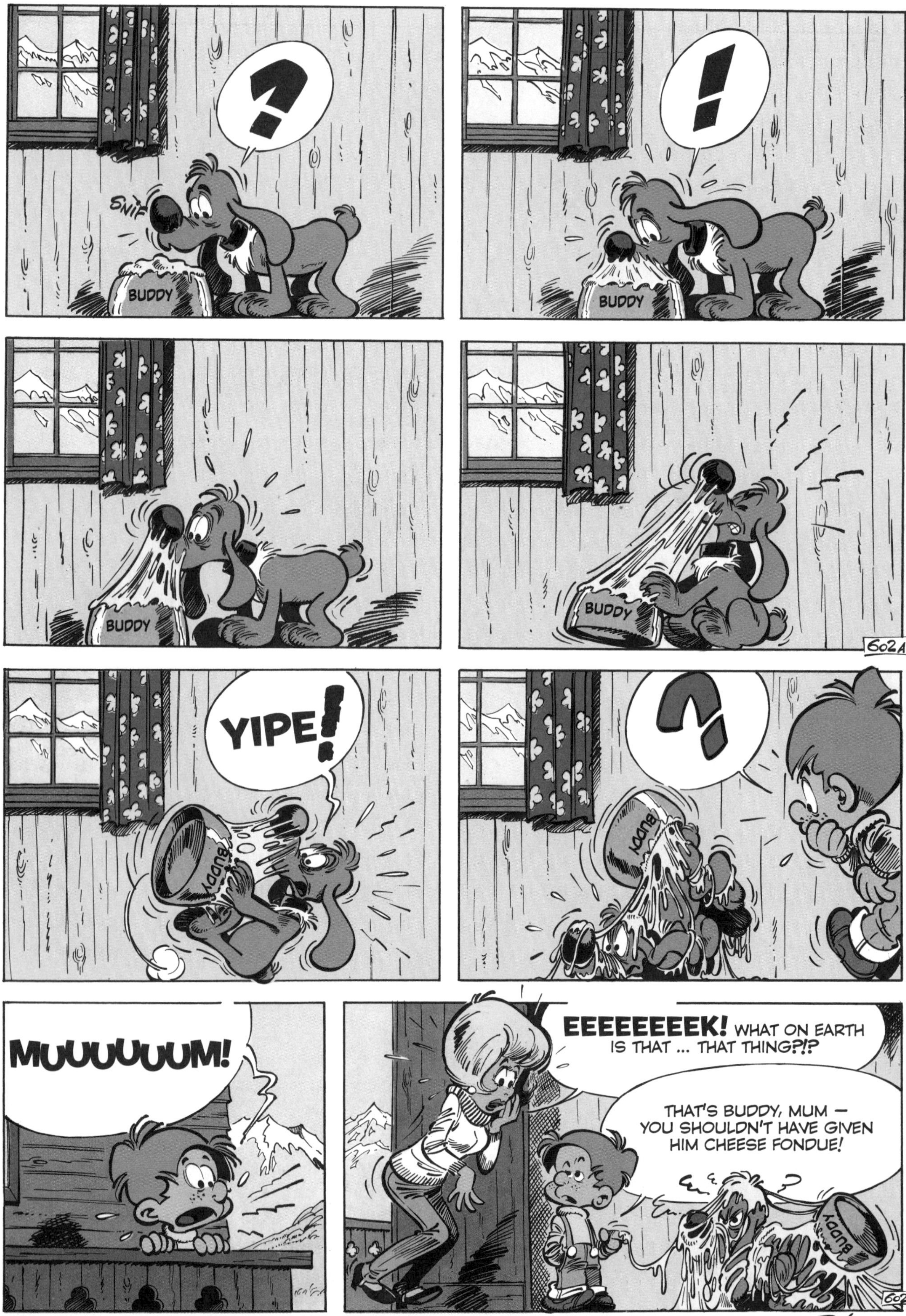

?
SNIF
BUDDY
!
BUDDY
BUDDY
BUDDY
602A
YIPE!
BUDDY
?
BUDDY
MUUUUUUM!
EEEEEEEEK! WHAT ON EARTH IS THAT ... THAT THING?!?
THAT'S BUDDY, MUM — YOU SHOULDN'T HAVE GIVEN HIM CHEESE FONDUE!
BUDDY
602B
Roba

Echo

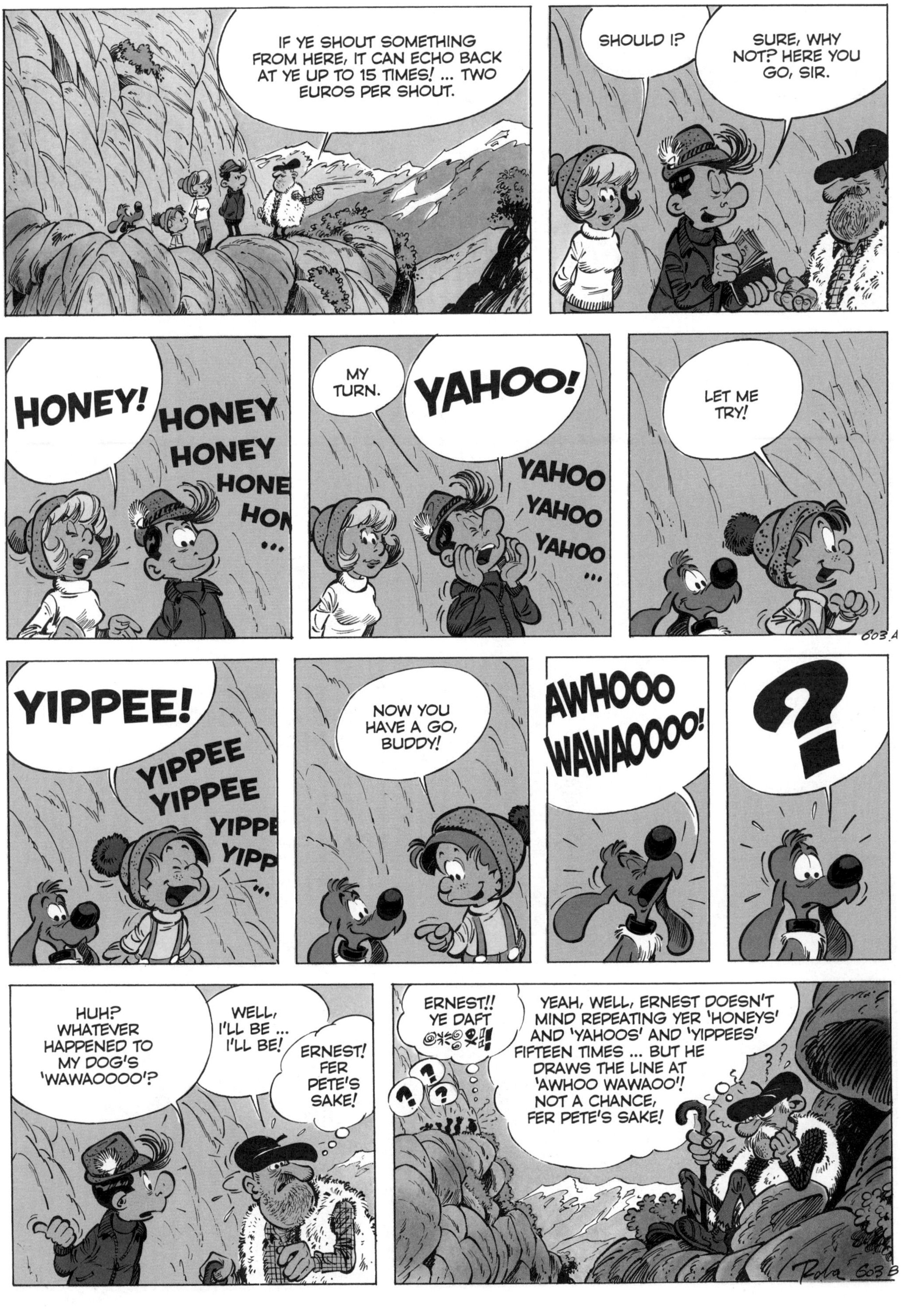

IF YE SHOUT SOMETHING FROM HERE, IT CAN ECHO BACK AT YE UP TO 15 TIMES! ... TWO EUROS PER SHOUT.
SHOULD I?
SURE, WHY NOT? HERE YOU GO, SIR.
HONEY!
HONEY HONEY HONE HON ...
MY TURN.
YAHOO!
YAHOO YAHOO YAHOO ...
LET ME TRY!
603 A
YIPPEE!
YIPPEE YIPPEE YIPPE YIPP ...
NOW YOU HAVE A GO, BUDDY!
AWHOOO WAWAOOOO!
?
HUH? WHATEVER HAPPENED TO MY DOG'S 'WAWAOOOO'?
WELL, I'LL BE ... I'LL BE!
ERNEST! FER PETE'S SAKE!
ERNEST!! YE DAFT
YEAH, WELL, ERNEST DOESN'T MIND REPEATING YER 'HONEYS' AND 'YAHOOS' AND 'YIPPEES' FIFTEEN TIMES ... BUT HE DRAWS THE LINE AT 'AWHOO WAWAOO'! NOT A CHANCE, FER PETE'S SAKE!
603 B

The Art of Baiting

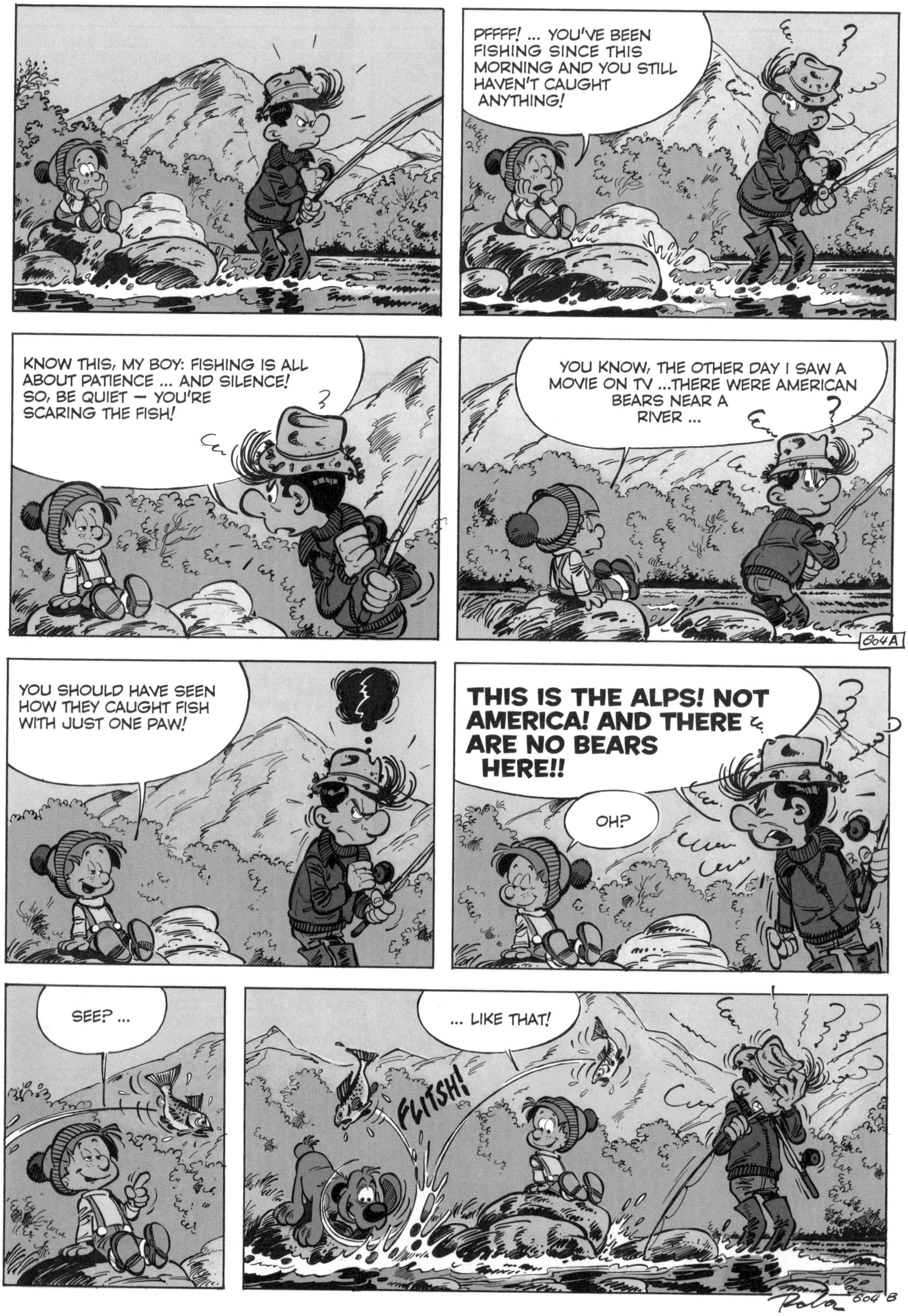
PFFFF! ... YOU'VE BEEN FISHING SINCE THIS MORNING AND YOU STILL HAVEN'T CAUGHT ANYTHING!
KNOW THIS, MY BOY: FISHING IS ALL ABOUT PATIENCE ... AND SILENCE! SO, BE QUIET — YOU'RE SCARING THE FISH!
YOU KNOW, THE OTHER DAY I SAW A MOVIE ON TV ...THERE WERE AMERICAN BEARS NEAR A RIVER ...
604A
YOU SHOULD HAVE SEEN HOW THEY CAUGHT FISH WITH JUST ONE PAW!
THIS IS THE ALPS! NOT AMERICA! AND THERE ARE NO BEARS HERE!!
OH?
SEE? ...
... LIKE THAT!
FLITSH!
Roba
604 B

Post Holidays Syndrome

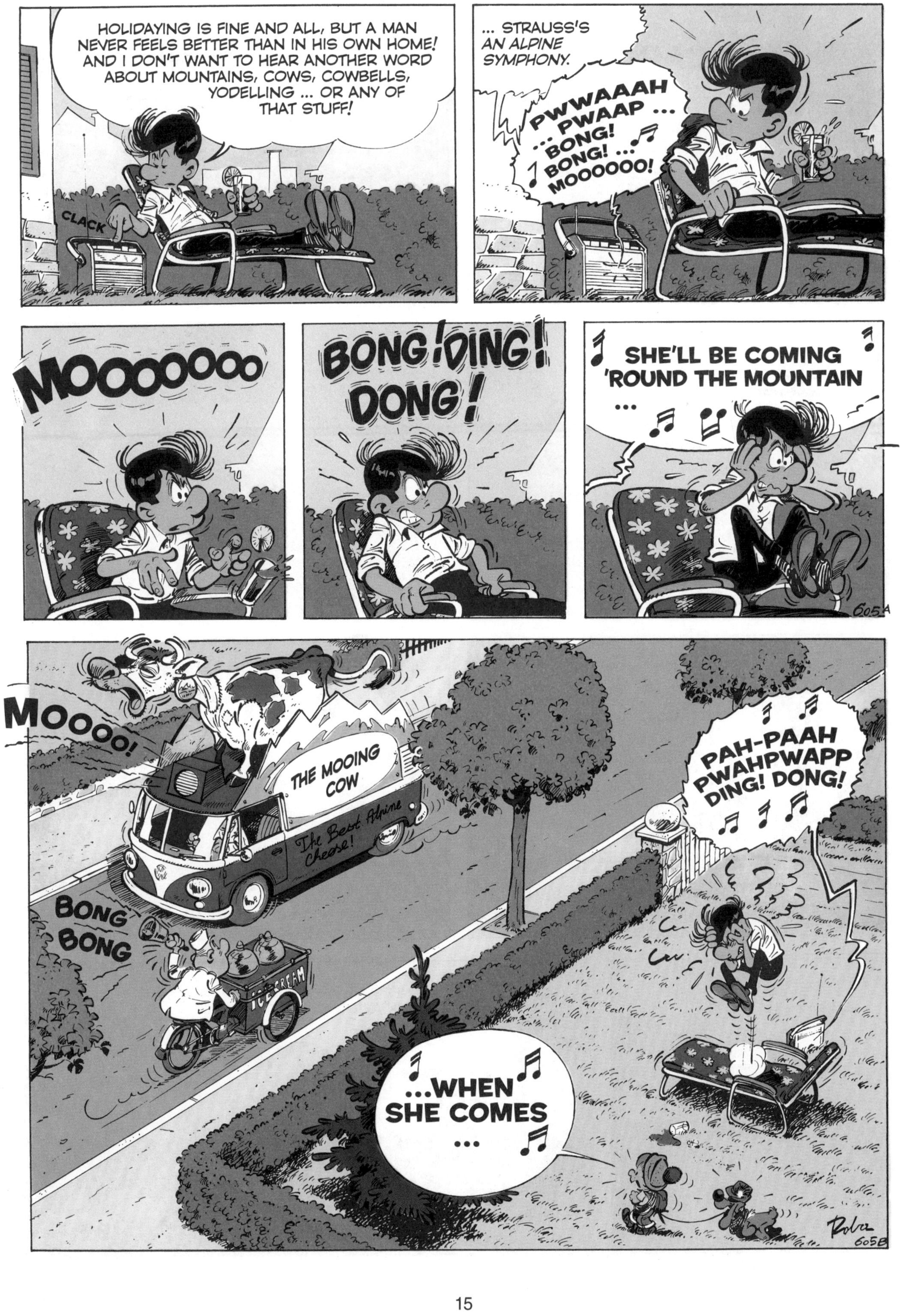
HOLIDAYING IS FINE AND ALL, BUT A MAN NEVER FEELS BETTER THAN IN HIS OWN HOME! AND I DON'T WANT TO HEAR ANOTHER WORD ABOUT MOUNTAINS, COWS, COWBELLS, YODELLING ... OR ANY OF THAT STUFF!
CLACK
... STRAUSS'S *AN ALPINE SYMPHONY.*
PWWAAAH ... PWAAP ... BONG! BONG! ... MOOOOOO!
MOOOOOOO
BONG! DING! DONG!
SHE'LL BE COMING 'ROUND THE MOUNTAIN ...
605A
MOOOO!
THE MOOING COW
The Best Alpine Cheese!
BONG BONG
ICE CREAM
PAH-PAAH PWAHPWAPP DING! DONG!
...WHEN SHE COMES ...
Roba
605B

Nature Abhors a Vacuum

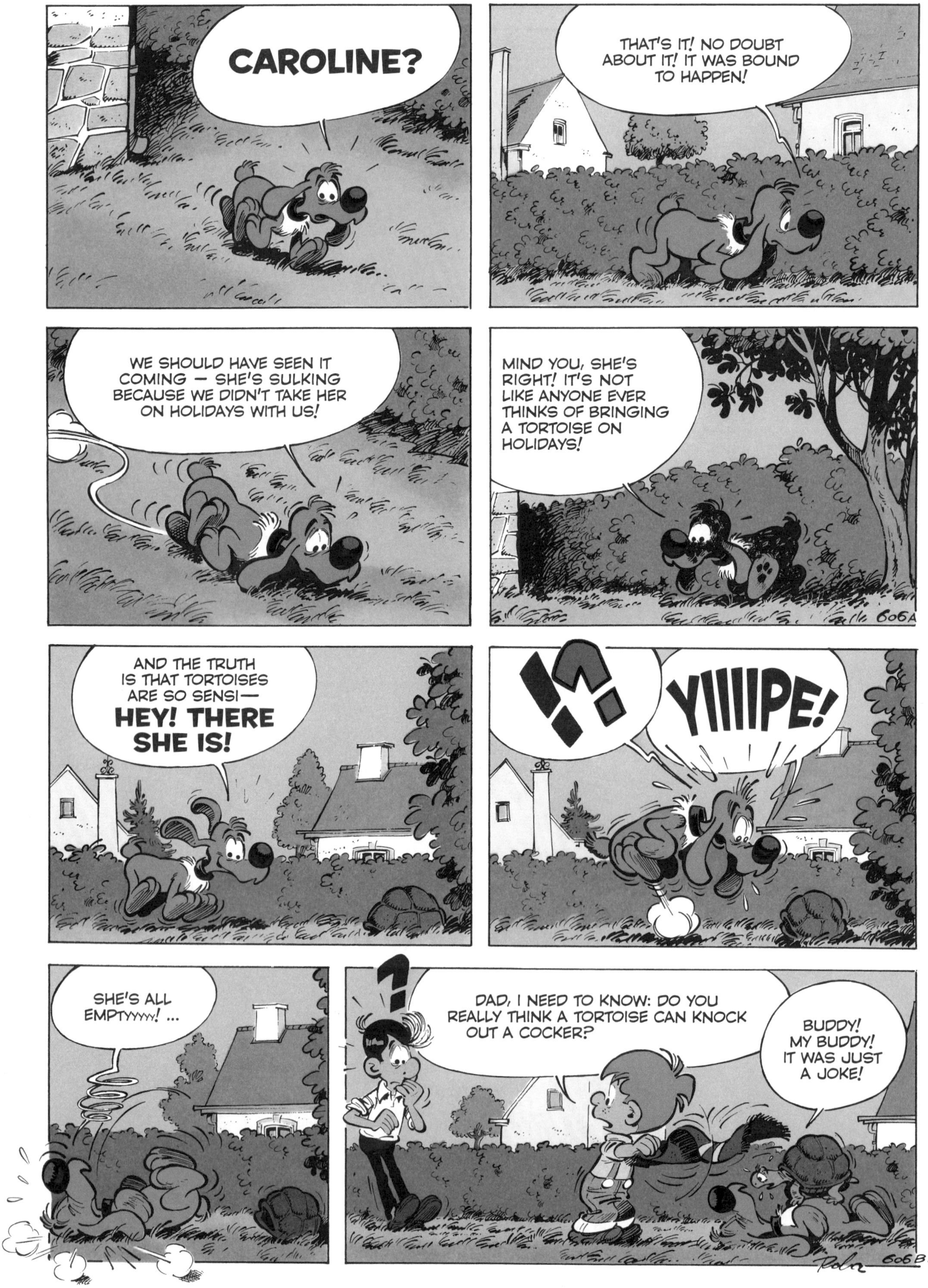

CAROLINE?
THAT'S IT! NO DOUBT ABOUT IT! IT WAS BOUND TO HAPPEN!
WE SHOULD HAVE SEEN IT COMING — SHE'S SULKING BECAUSE WE DIDN'T TAKE HER ON HOLIDAYS WITH US!
MIND YOU, SHE'S RIGHT! IT'S NOT LIKE ANYONE EVER THINKS OF BRINGING A TORTOISE ON HOLIDAYS!
AND THE TRUTH IS THAT TORTOISES ARE SO SENSI— HEY! THERE SHE IS!
!?
YIIIIPE!
SHE'S ALL EMPTYYYYY! ...
DAD, I NEED TO KNOW: DO YOU REALLY THINK A TORTOISE CAN KNOCK OUT A COCKER?
BUDDY! MY BUDDY! IT WAS JUST A JOKE!

Taking a Dip

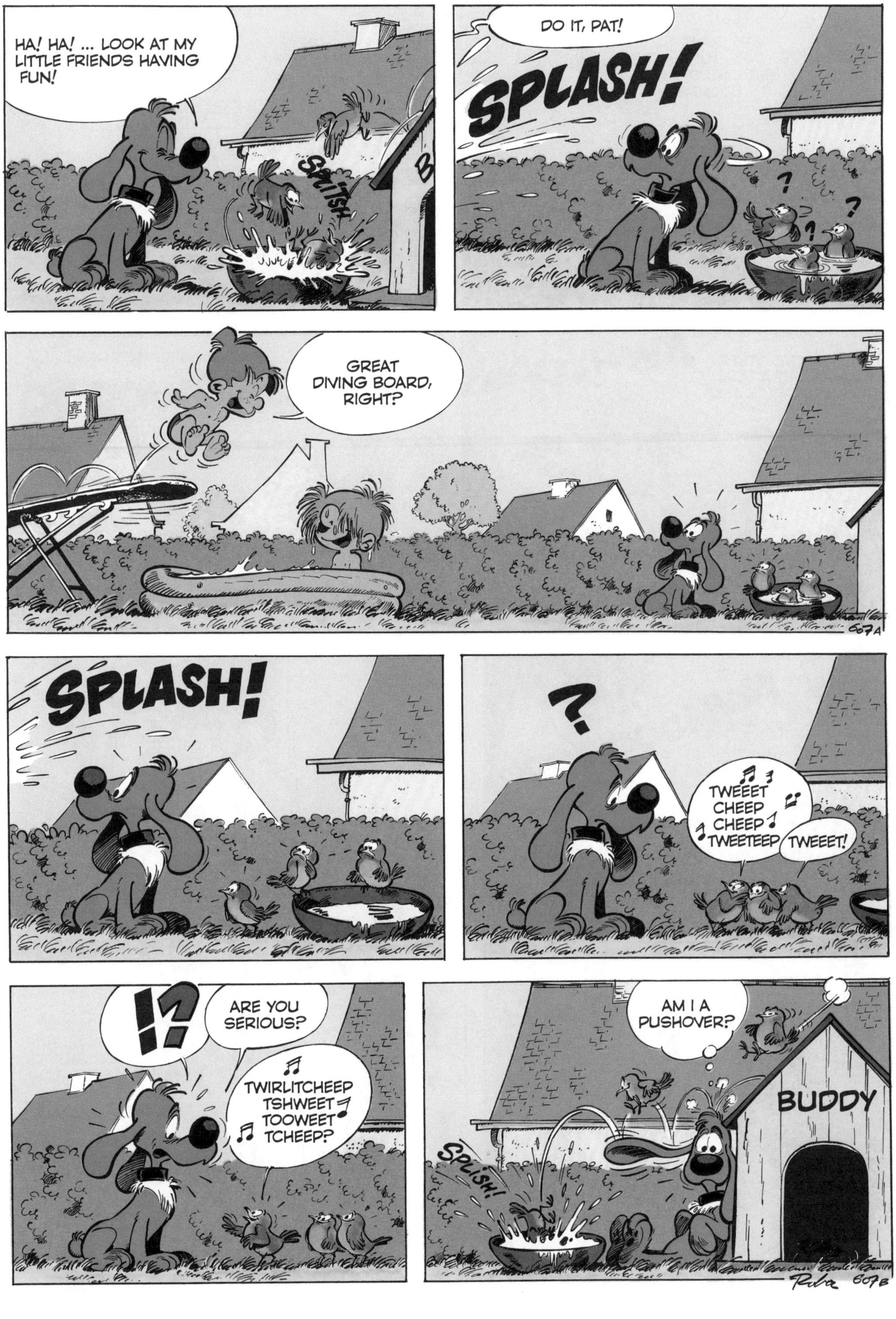
HA! HA! ... LOOK AT MY LITTLE FRIENDS HAVING FUN!
SPLITSH
DO IT, PAT!
SPLASH!
GREAT DIVING BOARD, RIGHT?
607A
SPLASH!
TWEEET CHEEP CHEEP TWEETEEP
TWEEET!
!?
ARE YOU SERIOUS?
TWIRLITCHEEP TSHWEET TOOWEET TCHEEP?
AM I A PUSHOVER?
BUDDY
SPLISH!
Roba 607B

Low Season

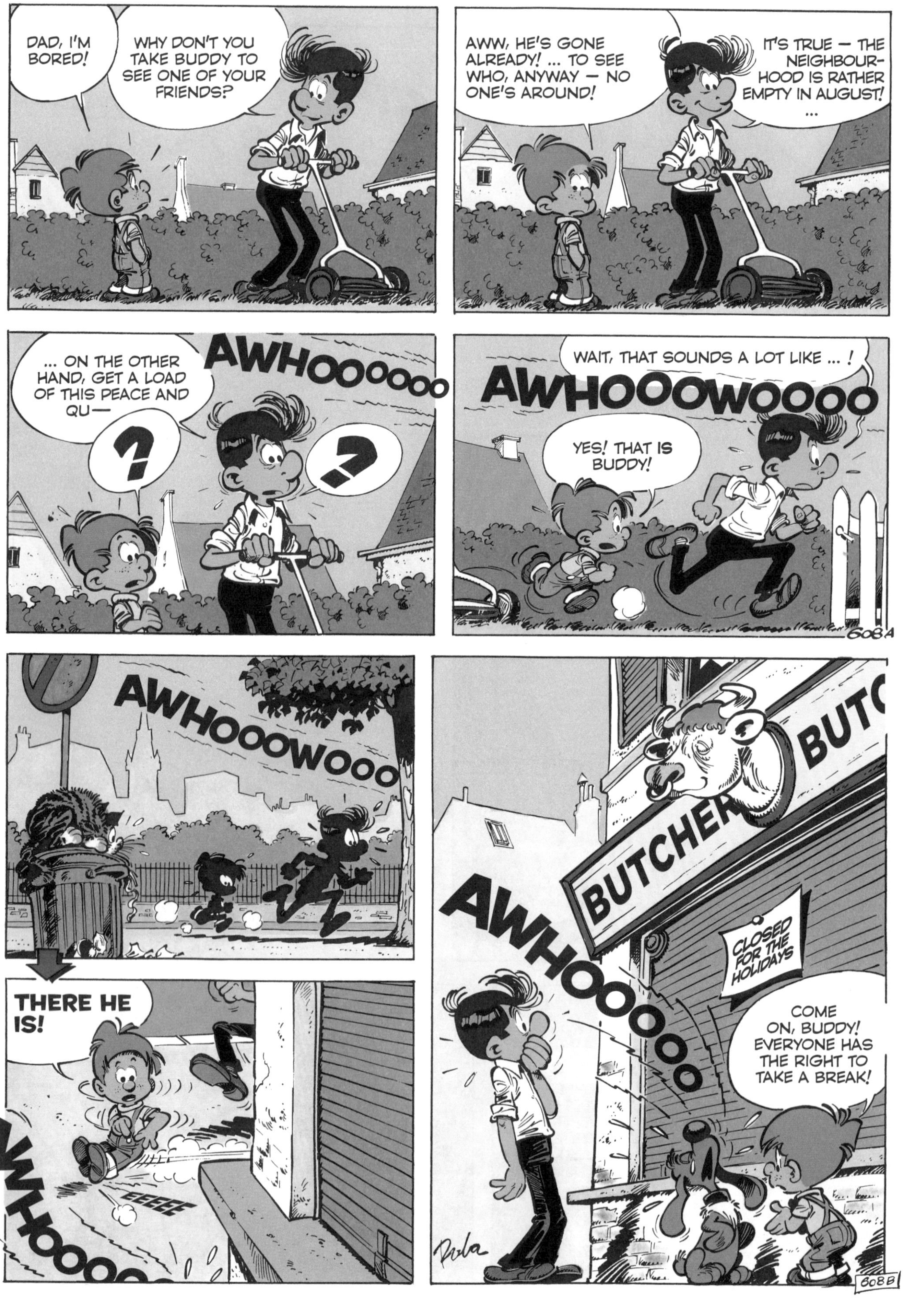
DAD, I'M BORED!
WHY DON'T YOU TAKE BUDDY TO SEE ONE OF YOUR FRIENDS?
AWW, HE'S GONE ALREADY! ... TO SEE WHO, ANYWAY — NO ONE'S AROUND!
IT'S TRUE — THE NEIGHBOURHOOD IS RATHER EMPTY IN AUGUST! ...
... ON THE OTHER HAND, GET A LOAD OF THIS PEACE AND QU—
AWHOOOOOO
?
?
WAIT, THAT SOUNDS A LOT LIKE ... !
AWHOOOWOOOO
YES! THAT IS BUDDY!
608 A
AWHOOOWOOO
THERE HE IS!
AWHOOOO
EEEEEE
BUTCHER
BUTC
CLOSED FOR THE HOLIDAYS
AWHOOOOOO
COME ON, BUDDY! EVERYONE HAS THE RIGHT TO TAKE A BREAK!
608 B

Drought

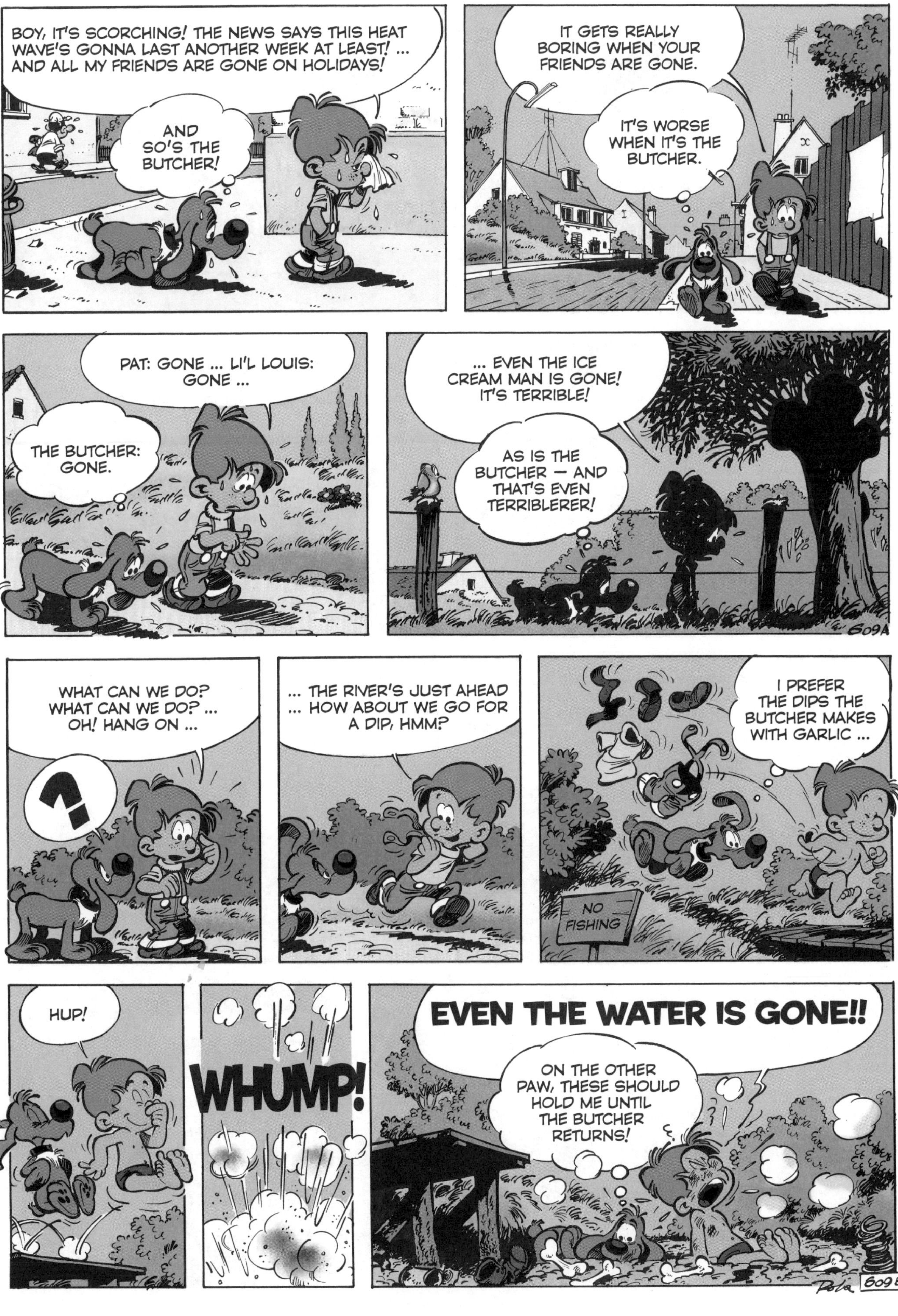

BOY, IT'S SCORCHING! THE NEWS SAYS THIS HEAT WAVE'S GONNA LAST ANOTHER WEEK AT LEAST! ... AND ALL MY FRIENDS ARE GONE ON HOLIDAYS!
AND SO'S THE BUTCHER!
IT GETS REALLY BORING WHEN YOUR FRIENDS ARE GONE.
IT'S WORSE WHEN IT'S THE BUTCHER.
PAT: GONE ... LI'L LOUIS: GONE ...
THE BUTCHER: GONE.
... EVEN THE ICE CREAM MAN IS GONE! IT'S TERRIBLE!
AS IS THE BUTCHER — AND THAT'S EVEN TERRIBLERER!
609A
WHAT CAN WE DO? WHAT CAN WE DO? ... OH! HANG ON ...
?
... THE RIVER'S JUST AHEAD ... HOW ABOUT WE GO FOR A DIP, HMM?
I PREFER THE DIPS THE BUTCHER MAKES WITH GARLIC ...
NO FISHING
HUP!
WHUMP!
EVEN THE WATER IS GONE!!
ON THE OTHER PAW, THESE SHOULD HOLD ME UNTIL THE BUTCHER RETURNS!
609B.

Hedge Knight

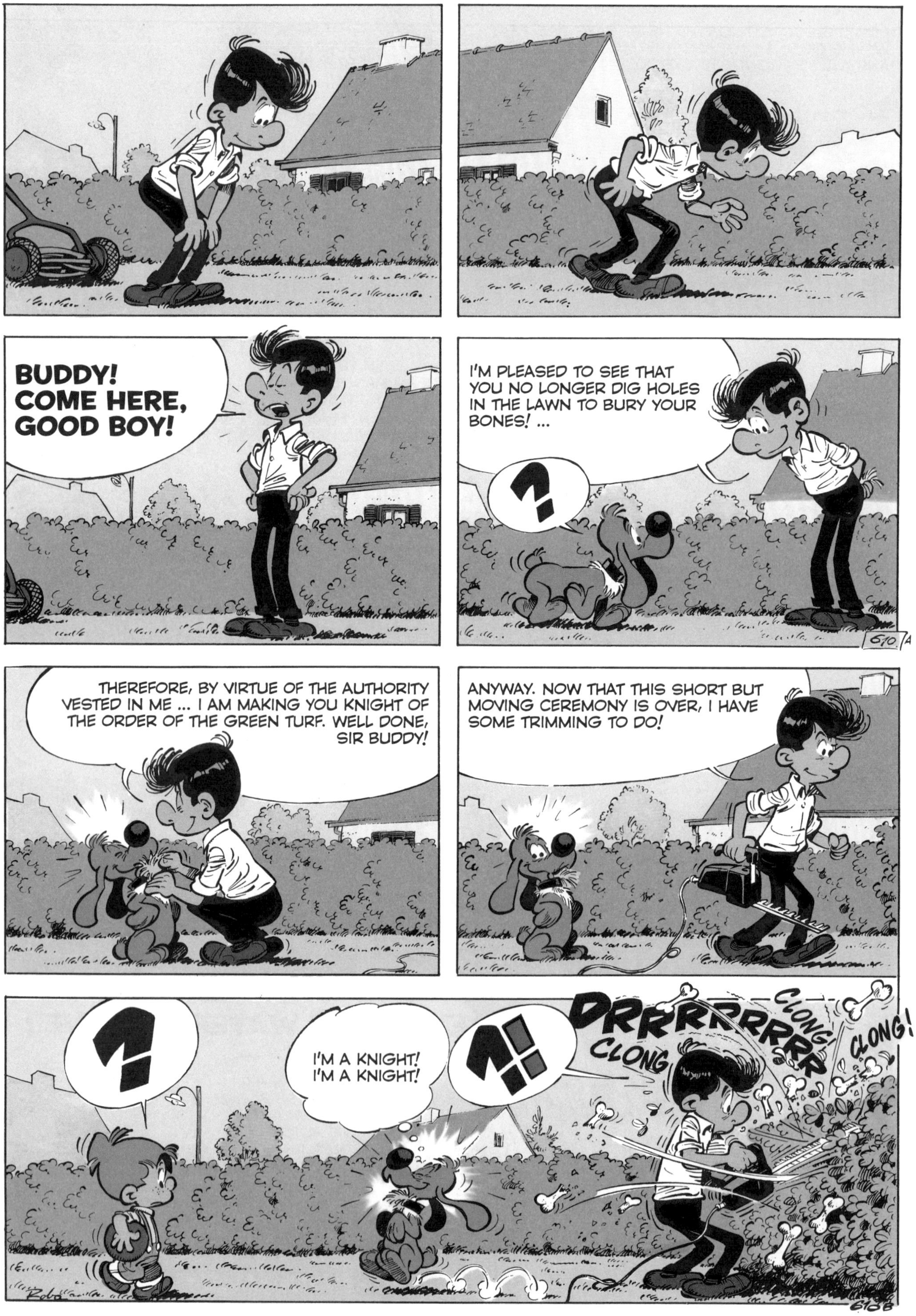

BUDDY! COME HERE, GOOD BOY!
I'M PLEASED TO SEE THAT YOU NO LONGER DIG HOLES IN THE LAWN TO BURY YOUR BONES! ...
?
THEREFORE, BY VIRTUE OF THE AUTHORITY VESTED IN ME ... I AM MAKING YOU KNIGHT OF THE ORDER OF THE GREEN TURF. WELL DONE, SIR BUDDY!
ANYWAY. NOW THAT THIS SHORT BUT MOVING CEREMONY IS OVER, I HAVE SOME TRIMMING TO DO!
?
I'M A KNIGHT! I'M A KNIGHT!
?!
DRRRRRRRRR
CLONG
CLONG!
CLONG!

Street Corner

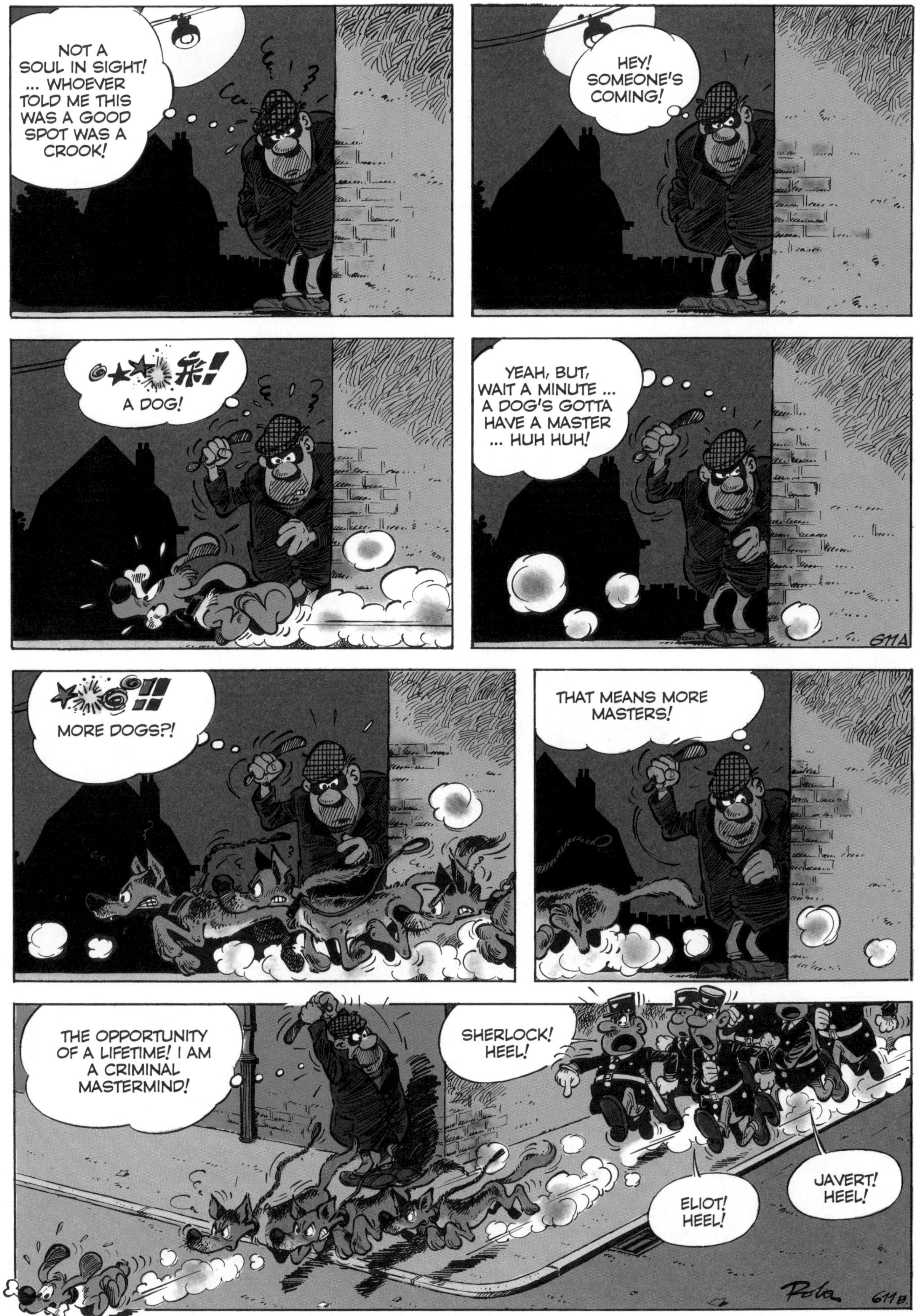

NOT A SOUL IN SIGHT! ... WHOEVER TOLD ME THIS WAS A GOOD SPOT WAS A CROOK!
HEY! SOMEONE'S COMING!
A DOG!
YEAH, BUT, WAIT A MINUTE ... A DOG'S GOTTA HAVE A MASTER ... HUH HUH!
MORE DOGS?!
THAT MEANS MORE MASTERS!
THE OPPORTUNITY OF A LIFETIME! I AM A CRIMINAL MASTERMIND!
SHERLOCK! HEEL!
ELIOT! HEEL!
JAVERT! HEEL!

Archery

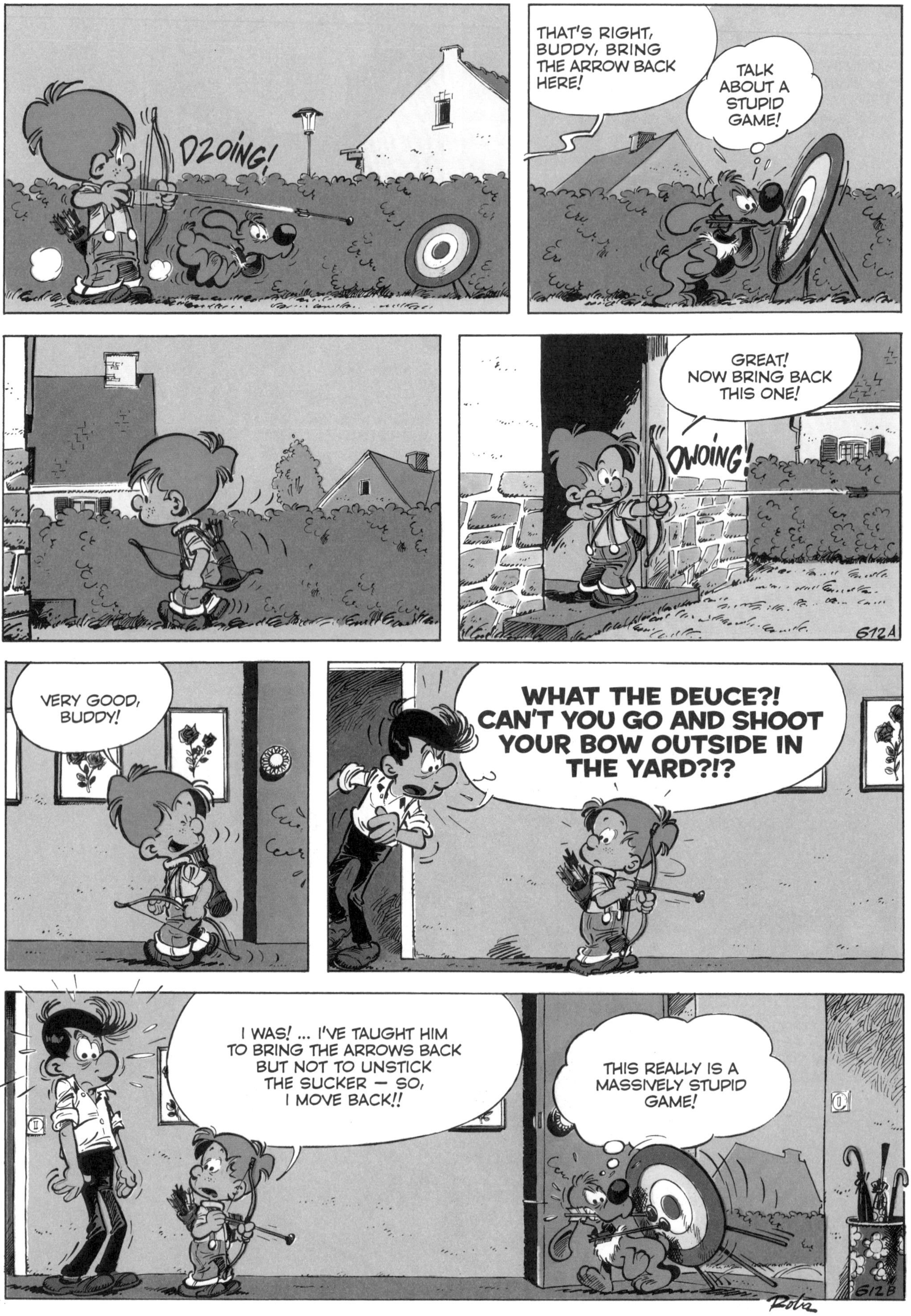
DZOING!
THAT'S RIGHT, BUDDY, BRING THE ARROW BACK HERE!
TALK ABOUT A STUPID GAME!
GREAT! NOW BRING BACK THIS ONE!
DWOING!
612 A
VERY GOOD, BUDDY!
WHAT THE DEUCE?! CAN'T YOU GO AND SHOOT YOUR BOW OUTSIDE IN THE YARD?!?
I WAS! ... I'VE TAUGHT HIM TO BRING THE ARROWS BACK BUT NOT TO UNSTICK THE SUCKER — SO, I MOVE BACK!!
THIS REALLY IS A MASSIVELY STUPID GAME!
612 B
Roba

Goodbye Kiss

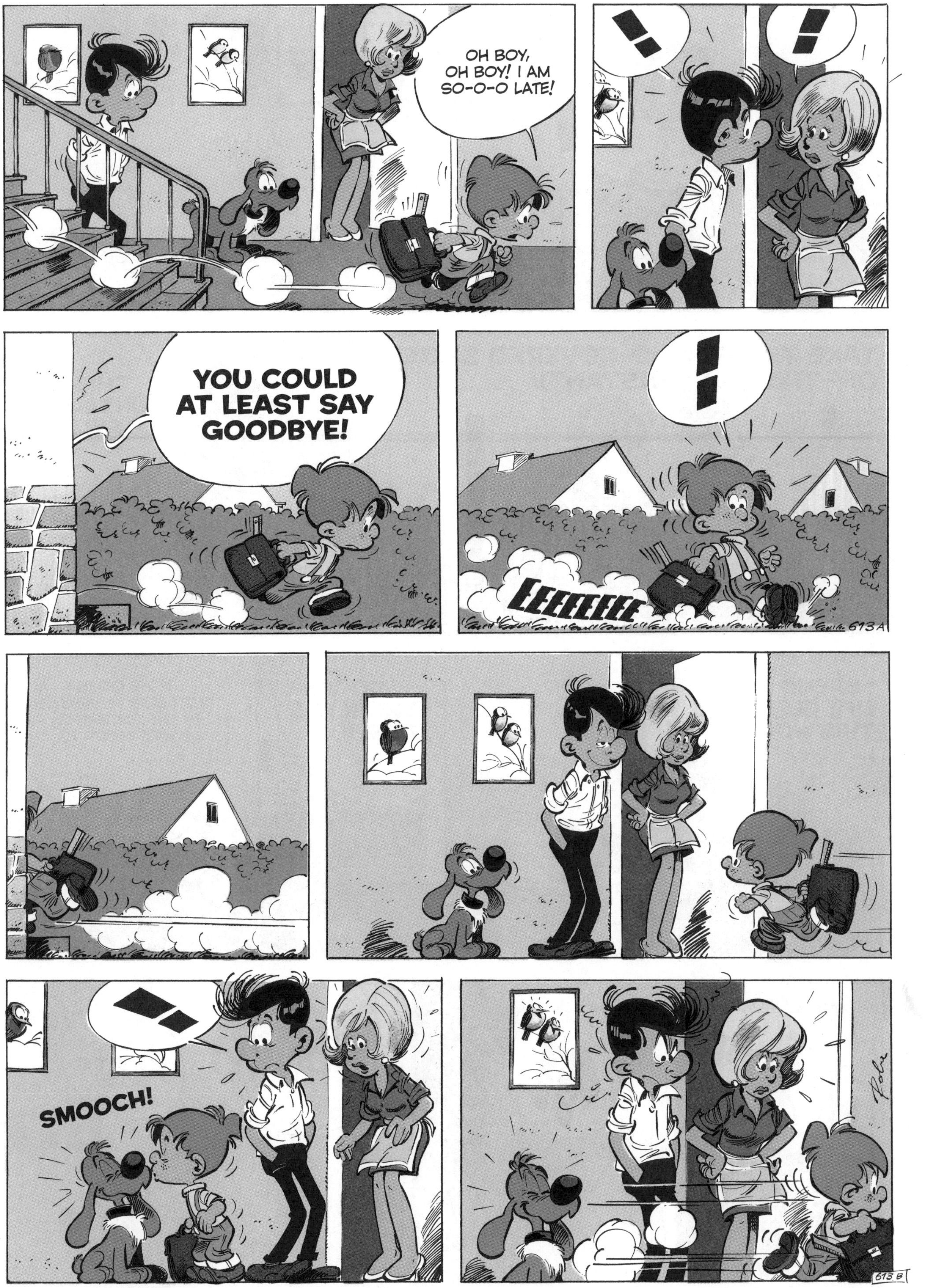
OH BOY, OH BOY! I AM SO-O-O LATE!
!
!
YOU COULD AT LEAST SAY GOODBYE!
!
EEEEEEEE
613 A
!
SMOOCH!
613 B

Filling Dad's Shoes

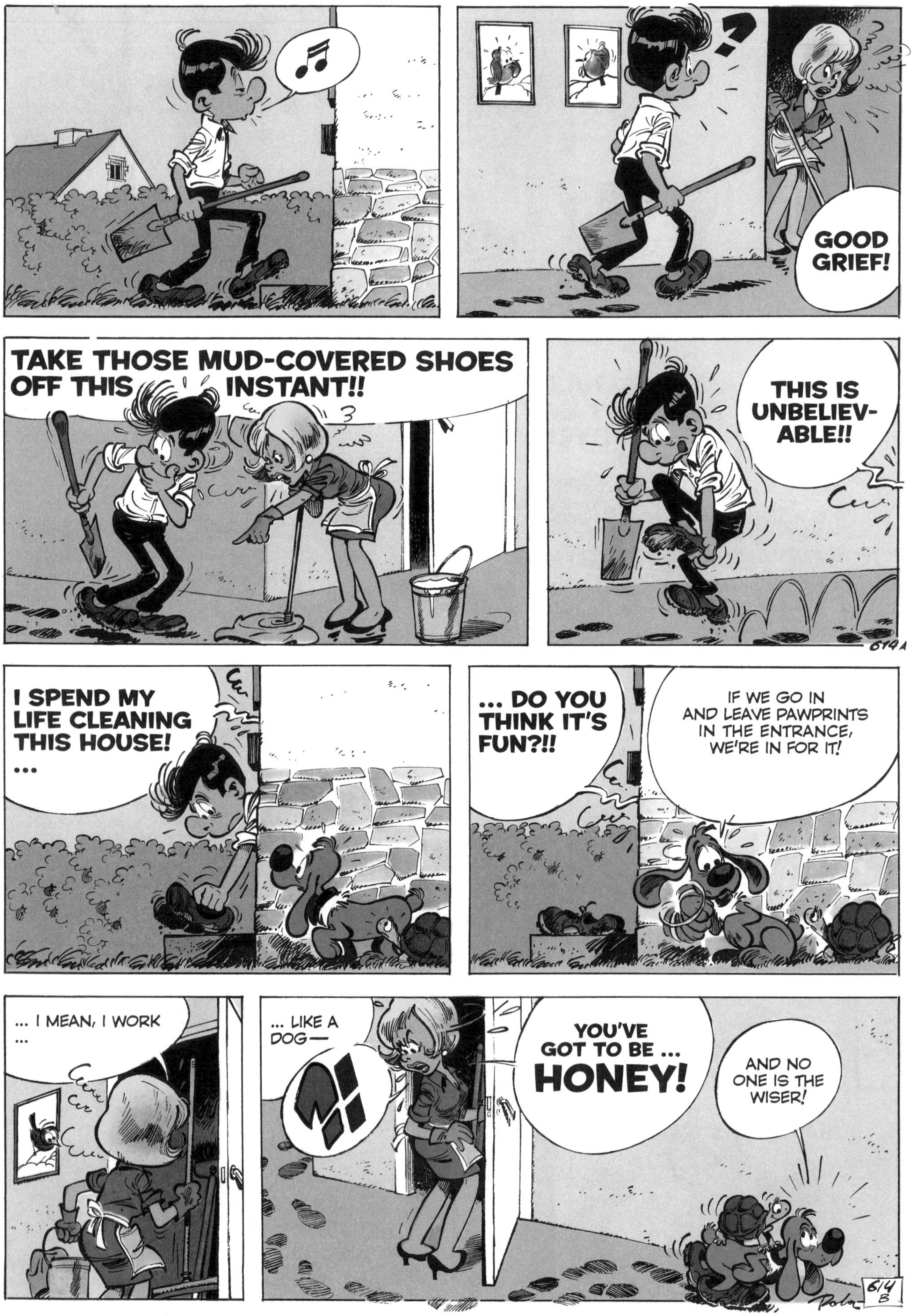
GOOD GRIEF!
TAKE THOSE MUD-COVERED SHOES OFF THIS INSTANT!!
THIS IS UNBELIEV-ABLE!!
614 A
I SPEND MY LIFE CLEANING THIS HOUSE! ...
... DO YOU THINK IT'S FUN?!!
IF WE GO IN AND LEAVE PAWPRINTS IN THE ENTRANCE, WE'RE IN FOR IT!
... I MEAN, I WORK ...
... LIKE A DOG—
YOU'VE GOT TO BE ... HONEY!
AND NO ONE IS THE WISER!
614 B

Train Problem

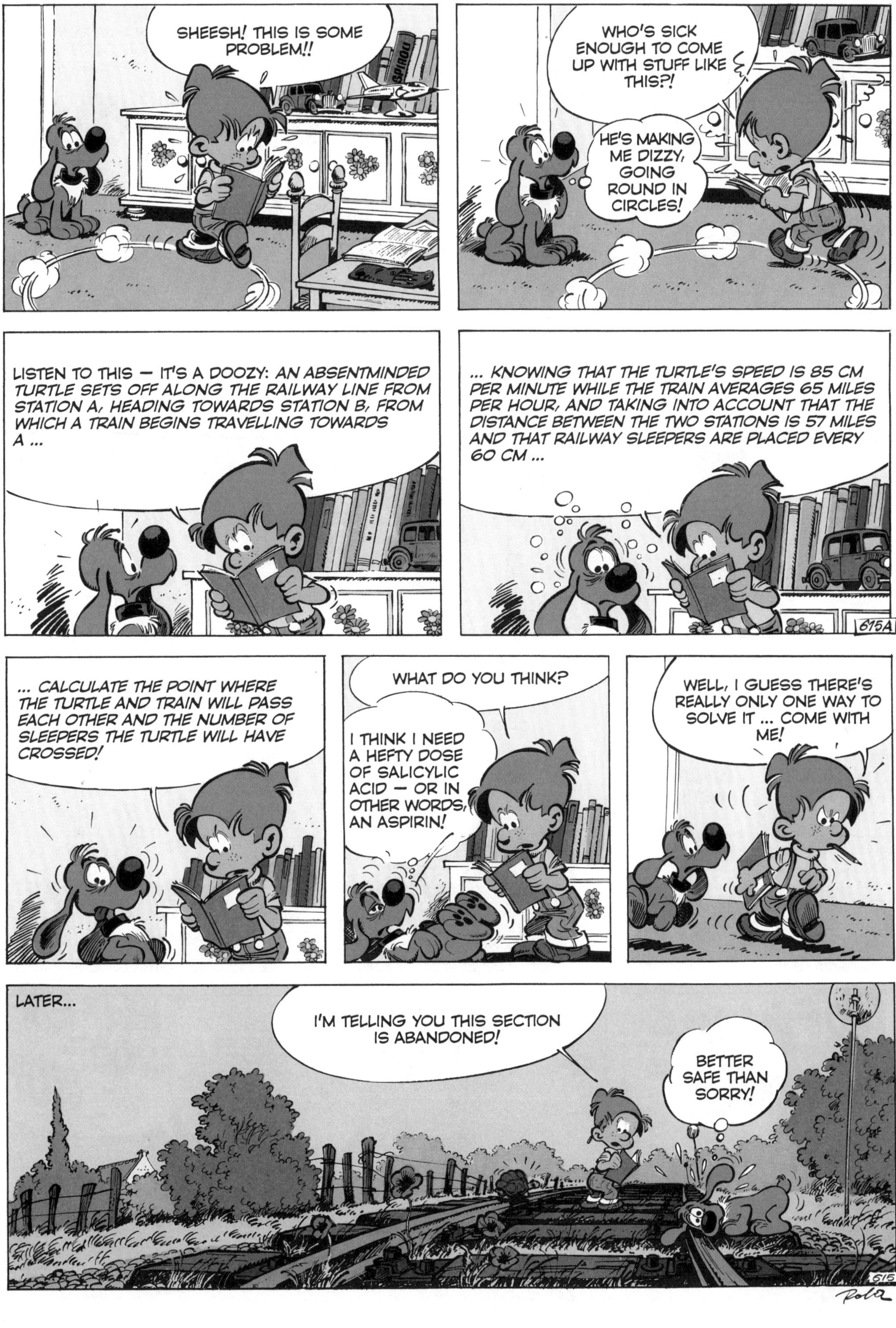
SHEESH! THIS IS SOME PROBLEM!!
WHO'S SICK ENOUGH TO COME UP WITH STUFF LIKE THIS?!
HE'S MAKING ME DIZZY, GOING ROUND IN CIRCLES!
LISTEN TO THIS — IT'S A DOOZY: AN ABSENTMINDED TURTLE SETS OFF ALONG THE RAILWAY LINE FROM STATION A, HEADING TOWARDS STATION B, FROM WHICH A TRAIN BEGINS TRAVELLING TOWARDS A ...
... KNOWING THAT THE TURTLE'S SPEED IS 85 CM PER MINUTE WHILE THE TRAIN AVERAGES 65 MILES PER HOUR, AND TAKING INTO ACCOUNT THAT THE DISTANCE BETWEEN THE TWO STATIONS IS 57 MILES AND THAT RAILWAY SLEEPERS ARE PLACED EVERY 60 CM ...
... CALCULATE THE POINT WHERE THE TURTLE AND TRAIN WILL PASS EACH OTHER AND THE NUMBER OF SLEEPERS THE TURTLE WILL HAVE CROSSED!
WHAT DO YOU THINK?
I THINK I NEED A HEFTY DOSE OF SALICYLIC ACID — OR IN OTHER WORDS, AN ASPIRIN!
WELL, I GUESS THERE'S REALLY ONLY ONE WAY TO SOLVE IT ... COME WITH ME!
LATER...
I'M TELLING YOU THIS SECTION IS ABANDONED!
BETTER SAFE THAN SORRY!

Taxation

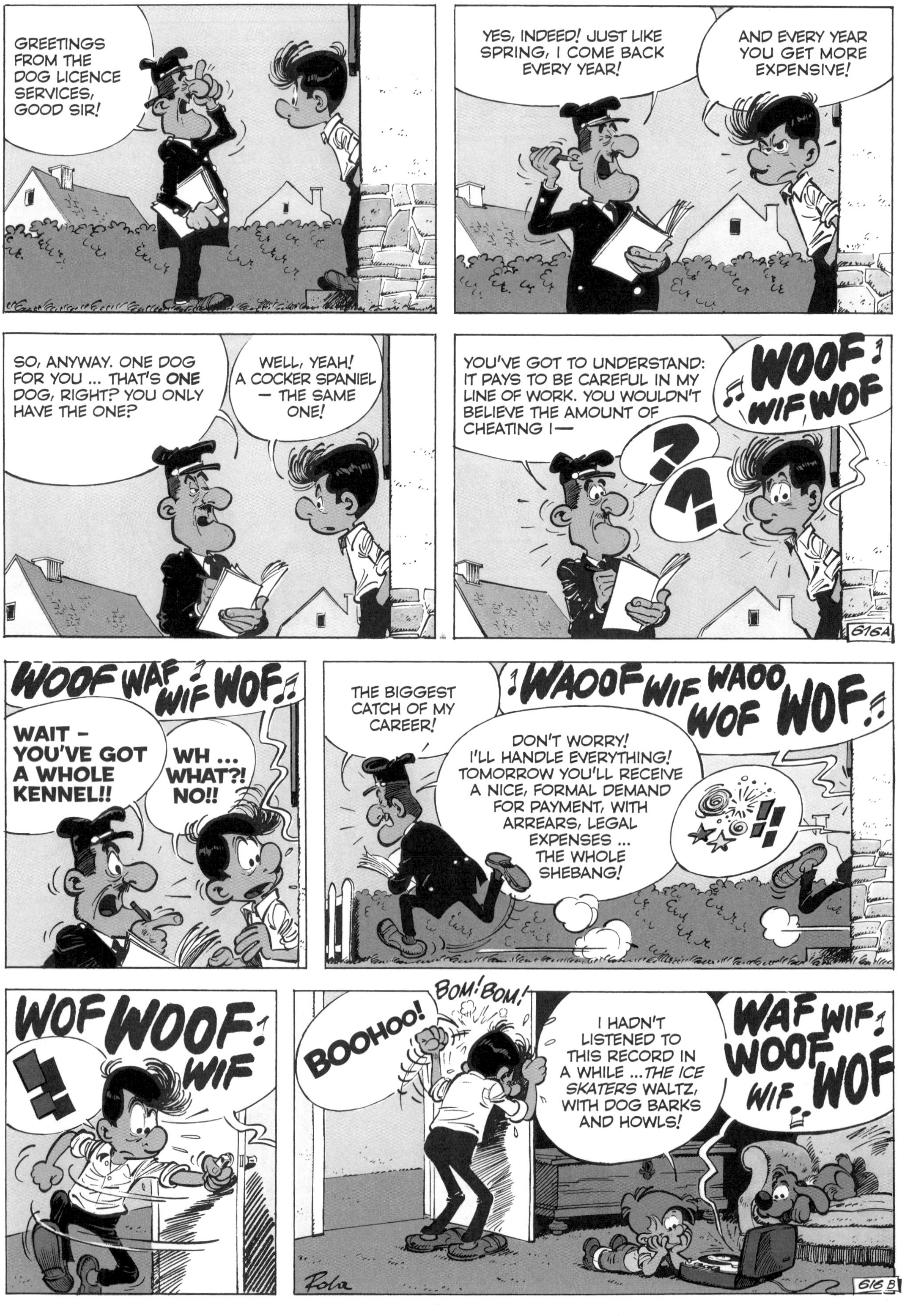

GREETINGS FROM THE DOG LICENCE SERVICES, GOOD SIR!
YES, INDEED! JUST LIKE SPRING, I COME BACK EVERY YEAR!
AND EVERY YEAR YOU GET MORE EXPENSIVE!
SO, ANYWAY. ONE DOG FOR YOU ... THAT'S **ONE** DOG, RIGHT? YOU ONLY HAVE THE ONE?
WELL, YEAH! A COCKER SPANIEL — THE SAME ONE!
YOU'VE GOT TO UNDERSTAND: IT PAYS TO BE CAREFUL IN MY LINE OF WORK. YOU WOULDN'T BELIEVE THE AMOUNT OF CHEATING I—
WOOF WIF WOF
?
?
616A
WOOF WAF WIF WOF
WAIT - YOU'VE GOT A WHOLE KENNEL!!
WH ... WHAT?! NO!!
THE BIGGEST CATCH OF MY CAREER!
WAOOF WIF WAOO WOF WOF
DON'T WORRY! I'LL HANDLE EVERYTHING! TOMORROW YOU'LL RECEIVE A NICE, FORMAL DEMAND FOR PAYMENT, WITH ARREARS, LEGAL EXPENSES ... THE WHOLE SHEBANG!
WOF WOOF WIF
BOOHOO!
BOM! BOM!
I HADN'T LISTENED TO THIS RECORD IN A WHILE ... *THE ICE SKATERS WALTZ*, WITH DOG BARKS AND HOWLS!
WAF WIF WOOF WIF WOF
Roba
616 B

Shyness

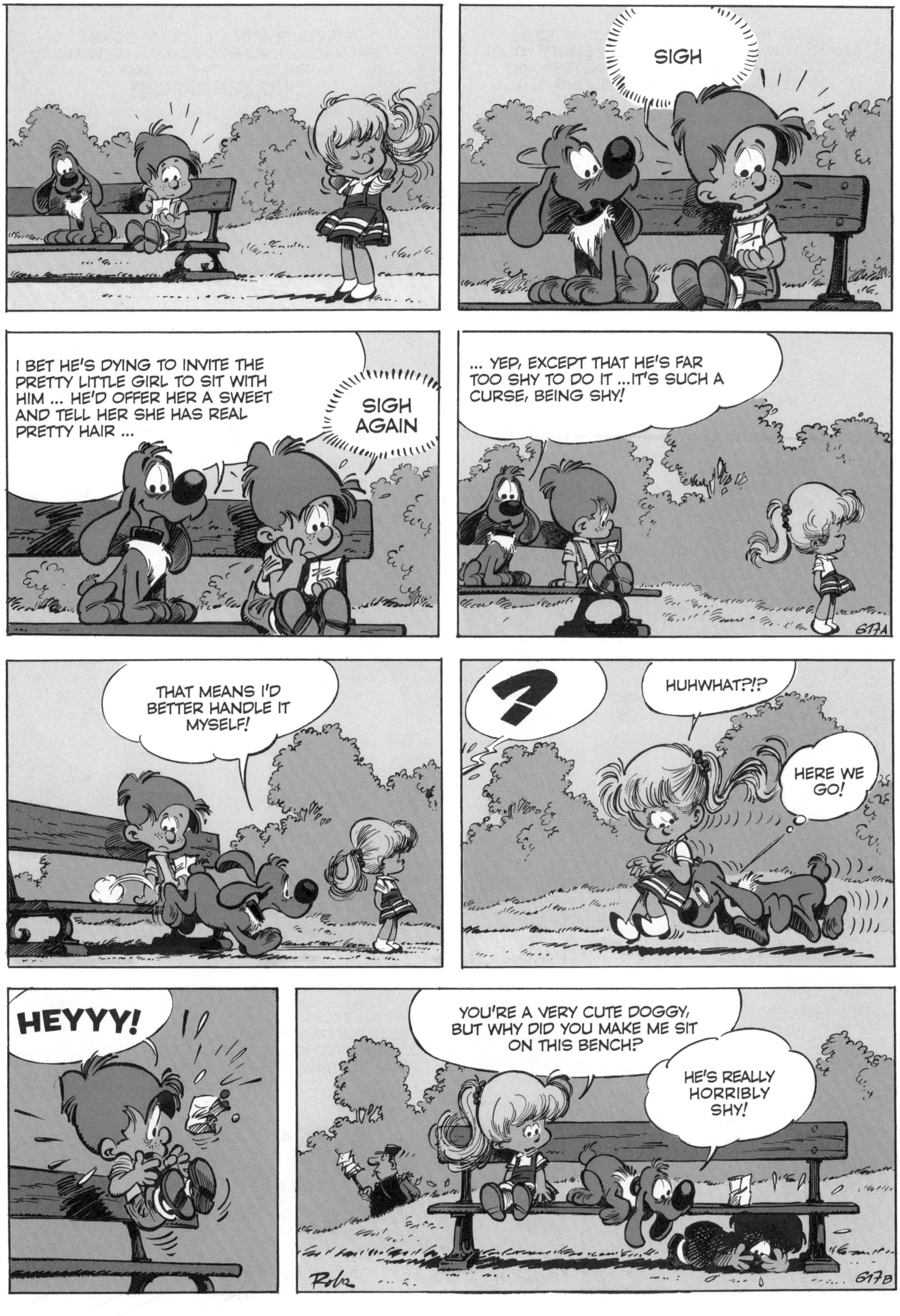
SIGH
I BET HE'S DYING TO INVITE THE PRETTY LITTLE GIRL TO SIT WITH HIM ... HE'D OFFER HER A SWEET AND TELL HER SHE HAS REAL PRETTY HAIR ...
SIGH AGAIN
... YEP, EXCEPT THAT HE'S FAR TOO SHY TO DO IT ...IT'S SUCH A CURSE, BEING SHY!
THAT MEANS I'D BETTER HANDLE IT MYSELF!
?
HUHWHAT?!?
HERE WE GO!
HEYYY!
YOU'RE A VERY CUTE DOGGY, BUT WHY DID YOU MAKE ME SIT ON THIS BENCH?
HE'S REALLY HORRIBLY SHY!

Taking Stock

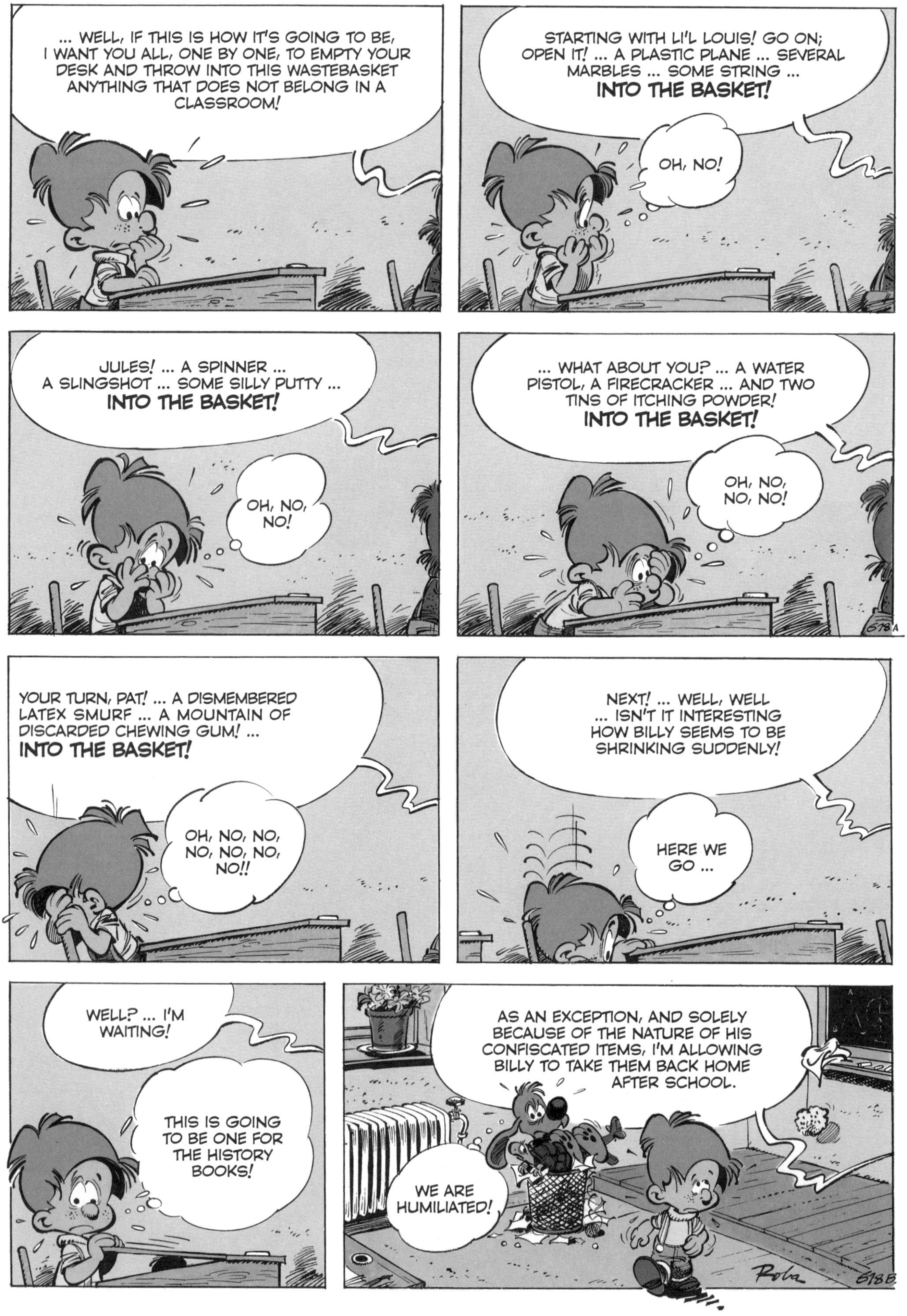

... WELL, IF THIS IS HOW IT'S GOING TO BE, I WANT YOU ALL, ONE BY ONE, TO EMPTY YOUR DESK AND THROW INTO THIS WASTEBASKET ANYTHING THAT DOES NOT BELONG IN A CLASSROOM!
STARTING WITH LI'L LOUIS! GO ON; OPEN IT! ... A PLASTIC PLANE ... SEVERAL MARBLES ... SOME STRING ... **INTO THE BASKET!**
OH, NO!
JULES! ... A SPINNER ... A SLINGSHOT ... SOME SILLY PUTTY ... **INTO THE BASKET!**
OH, NO, NO!
... WHAT ABOUT YOU? ... A WATER PISTOL, A FIRECRACKER ... AND TWO TINS OF ITCHING POWDER! **INTO THE BASKET!**
OH, NO, NO, NO!
YOUR TURN, PAT! ... A DISMEMBERED LATEX SMURF ... A MOUNTAIN OF DISCARDED CHEWING GUM! ... **INTO THE BASKET!**
OH, NO, NO, NO, NO, NO, NO!!
NEXT! ... WELL, WELL ... ISN'T IT INTERESTING HOW BILLY SEEMS TO BE SHRINKING SUDDENLY!
HERE WE GO ...
WELL? ... I'M WAITING!
THIS IS GOING TO BE ONE FOR THE HISTORY BOOKS!
AS AN EXCEPTION, AND SOLELY BECAUSE OF THE NATURE OF HIS CONFISCATED ITEMS, I'M ALLOWING BILLY TO TAKE THEM BACK HOME AFTER SCHOOL.
WE ARE HUMILIATED!
Roba

That Old Chestnut

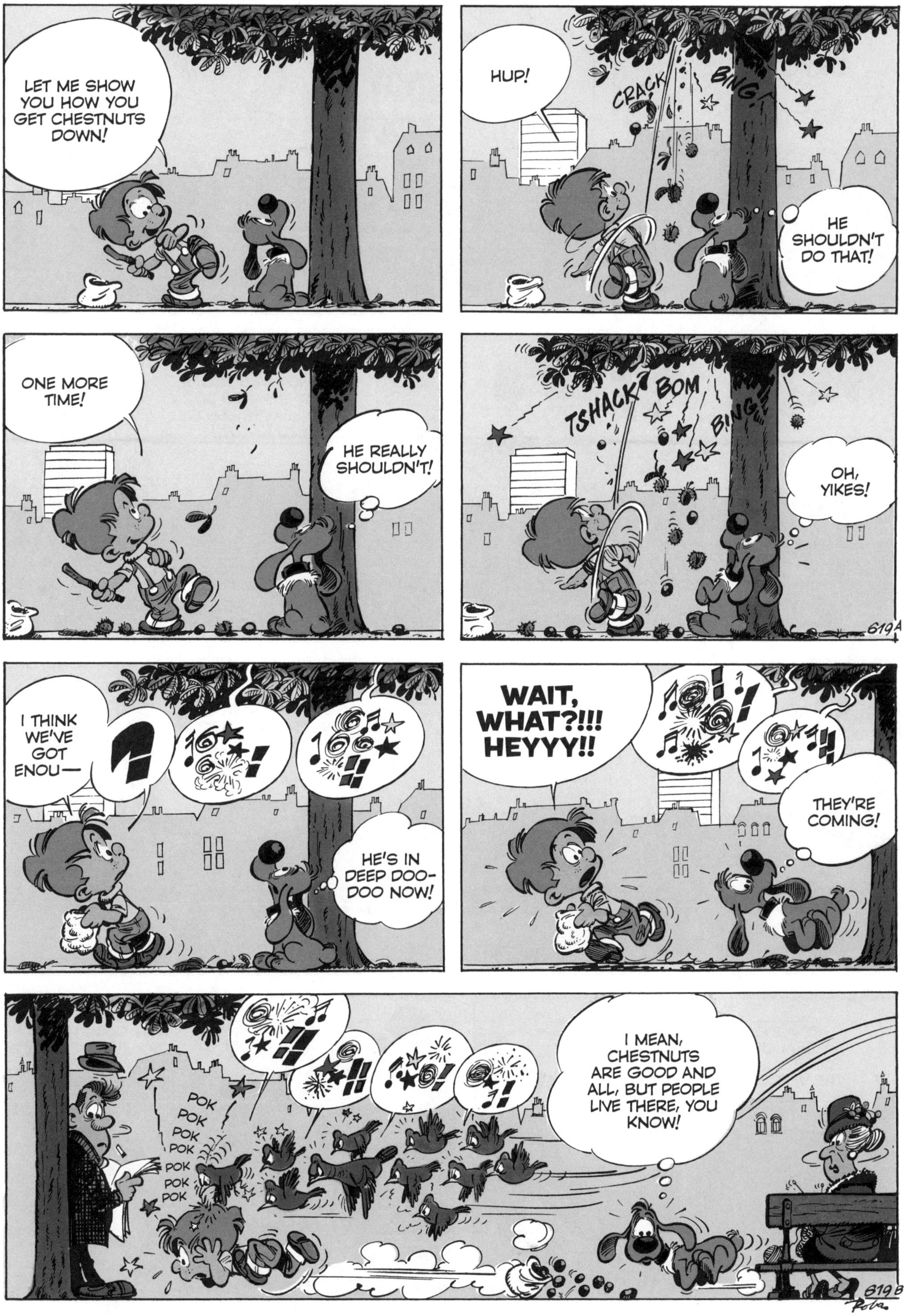

LET ME SHOW YOU HOW YOU GET CHESTNUTS DOWN!
HUP!
CRACK
BING
HE SHOULDN'T DO THAT!
ONE MORE TIME!
HE REALLY SHOULDN'T!
TSHACK
BOM
BING
OH, YIKES!
619 A
I THINK WE'VE GOT ENOU—
HE'S IN DEEP DOO-DOO NOW!
WAIT, WHAT?!!! HEYYY!!
THEY'RE COMING!
POK
POK
POK
POK
POK
POK
POK
I MEAN, CHESTNUTS ARE GOOD AND ALL, BUT PEOPLE LIVE THERE, YOU KNOW!
619 B
Roba

Low Cuisine

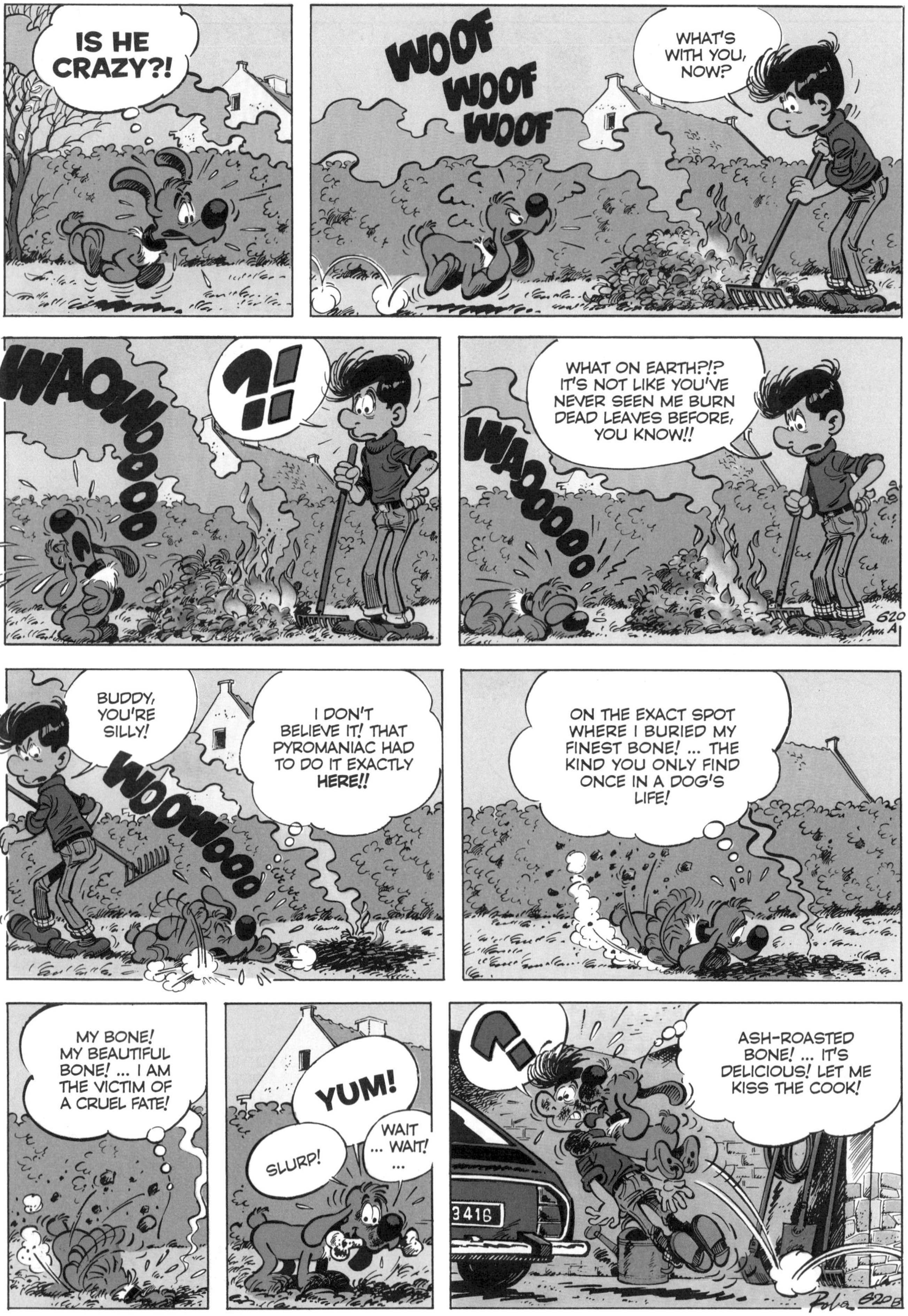
IS HE CRAZY?!
WOOF WOOF WOOF
WHAT'S WITH YOU, NOW?
WAOWOOOOO
?!
WHAT ON EARTH?!? IT'S NOT LIKE YOU'VE NEVER SEEN ME BURN DEAD LEAVES BEFORE, YOU KNOW!!
WAOOOOOO
BUDDY, YOU'RE SILLY!
WOOWOOO
I DON'T BELIEVE IT! THAT PYROMANIAC HAD TO DO IT EXACTLY **HERE!!**
ON THE EXACT SPOT WHERE I BURIED MY FINEST BONE! ... THE KIND YOU ONLY FIND ONCE IN A DOG'S LIFE!
MY BONE! MY BEAUTIFUL BONE! ... I AM THE VICTIM OF A CRUEL FATE!
YUM!
SLURP!
WAIT ... WAIT! ...
?
ASH-ROASTED BONE! ... IT'S DELICIOUS! LET ME KISS THE COOK!

No Pane ...

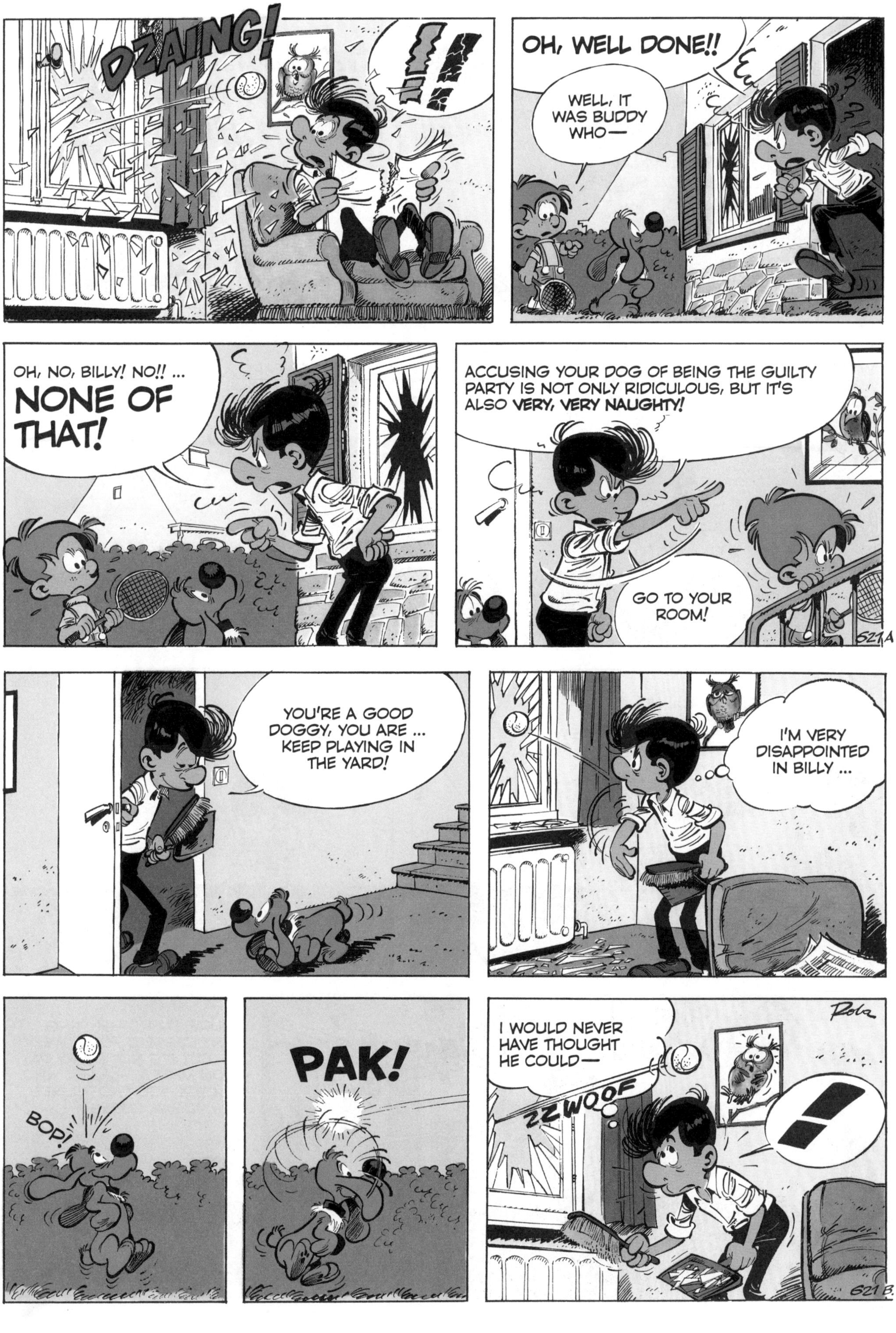
DZAING!
!!
OH, WELL DONE!!
WELL, IT WAS BUDDY WHO—
OH, NO, BILLY! NO!! ... NONE OF THAT!
ACCUSING YOUR DOG OF BEING THE GUILTY PARTY IS NOT ONLY RIDICULOUS, BUT IT'S ALSO VERY, VERY NAUGHTY!
GO TO YOUR ROOM!
YOU'RE A GOOD DOGGY, YOU ARE ... KEEP PLAYING IN THE YARD!
I'M VERY DISAPPOINTED IN BILLY ...
BOP!
PAK!
I WOULD NEVER HAVE THOUGHT HE COULD—
ZZWOOF
!

… No Gain!

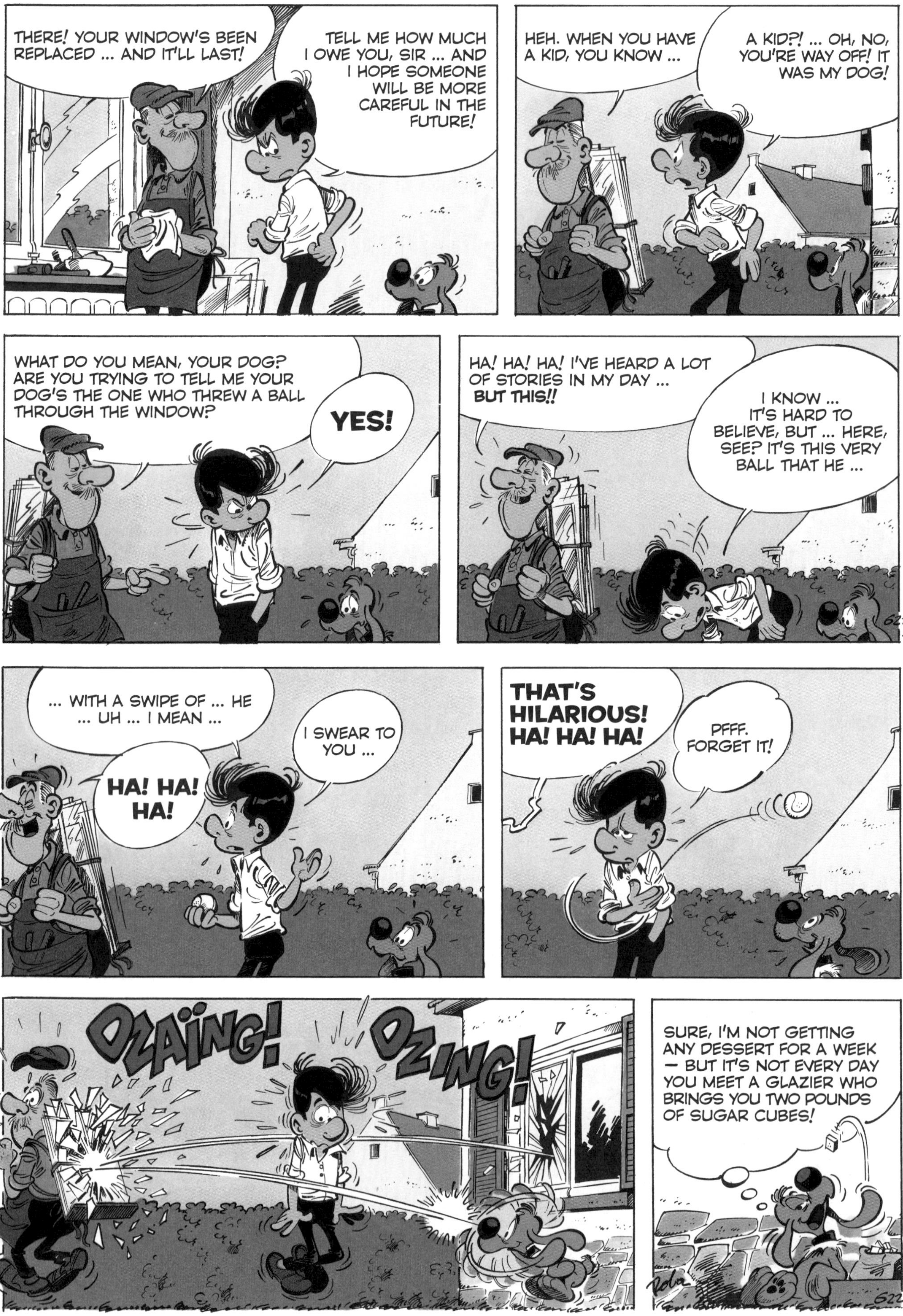
THERE! YOUR WINDOW'S BEEN REPLACED … AND IT'LL LAST!
TELL ME HOW MUCH I OWE YOU, SIR … AND I HOPE SOMEONE WILL BE MORE CAREFUL IN THE FUTURE!
HEH. WHEN YOU HAVE A KID, YOU KNOW …
A KID?! … OH, NO, YOU'RE WAY OFF! IT WAS MY DOG!
WHAT DO YOU MEAN, YOUR DOG? ARE YOU TRYING TO TELL ME YOUR DOG'S THE ONE WHO THREW A BALL THROUGH THE WINDOW?
YES!
HA! HA! HA! I'VE HEARD A LOT OF STORIES IN MY DAY … BUT THIS!!
I KNOW … IT'S HARD TO BELIEVE, BUT … HERE, SEE? IT'S THIS VERY BALL THAT HE …
… WITH A SWIPE OF … HE … UH … I MEAN …
HA! HA! HA!
I SWEAR TO YOU …
THAT'S HILARIOUS! HA! HA! HA!
PFFF. FORGET IT!
DZAÏNG!
DZING!
SURE, I'M NOT GETTING ANY DESSERT FOR A WEEK — BUT IT'S NOT EVERY DAY YOU MEET A GLAZIER WHO BRINGS YOU TWO POUNDS OF SUGAR CUBES!

High Fashion

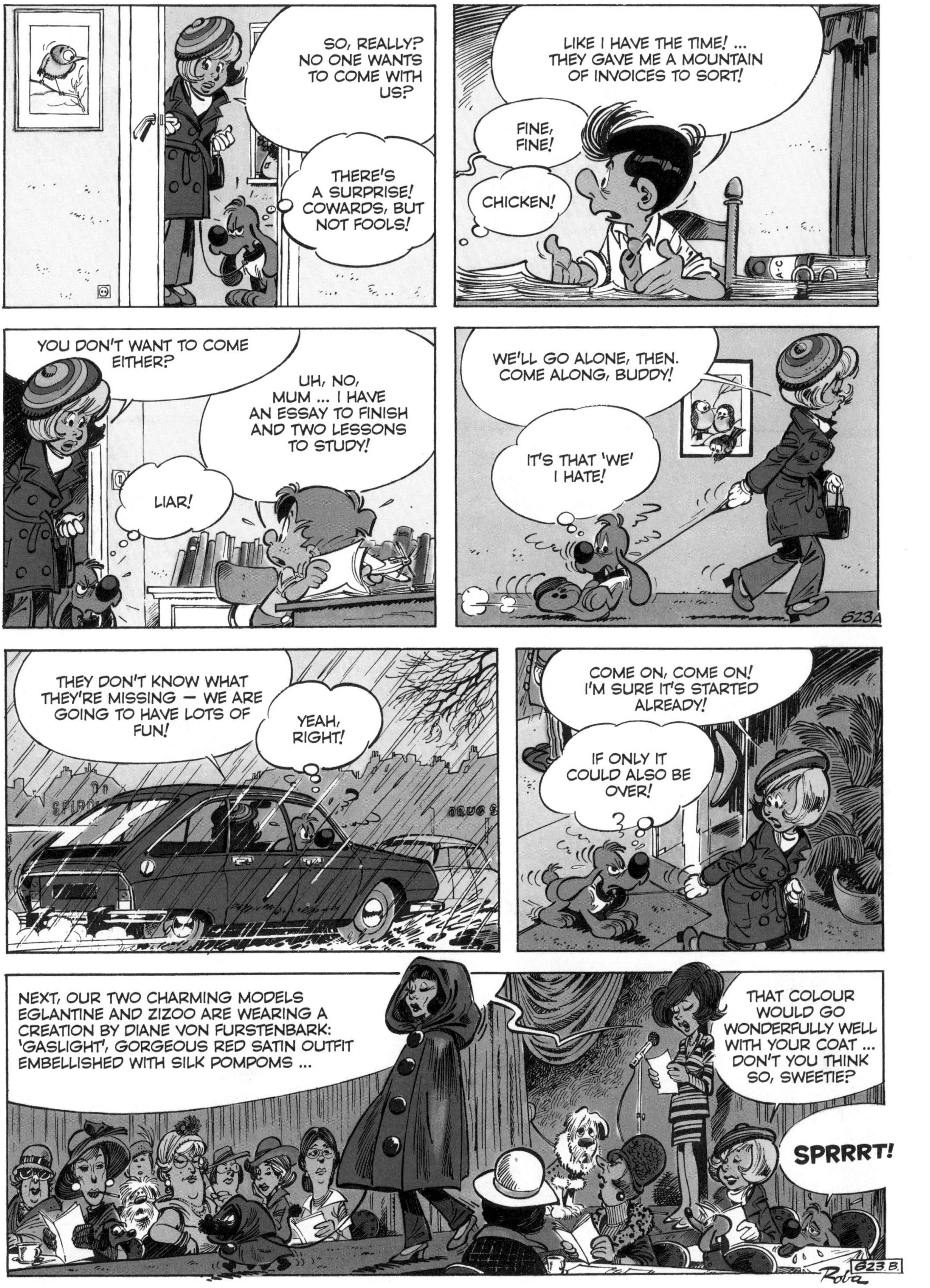
SO, REALLY? NO ONE WANTS TO COME WITH US?
THERE'S A SURPRISE! COWARDS, BUT NOT FOOLS!
LIKE I HAVE THE TIME! ... THEY GAVE ME A MOUNTAIN OF INVOICES TO SORT!
FINE, FINE!
CHICKEN!
YOU DON'T WANT TO COME EITHER?
UH, NO, MUM ... I HAVE AN ESSAY TO FINISH AND TWO LESSONS TO STUDY!
LIAR!
WE'LL GO ALONE, THEN. COME ALONG, BUDDY!
IT'S THAT 'WE' I HATE!
623A
THEY DON'T KNOW WHAT THEY'RE MISSING — WE ARE GOING TO HAVE LOTS OF FUN!
YEAH, RIGHT!
COME ON, COME ON! I'M SURE IT'S STARTED ALREADY!
IF ONLY IT COULD ALSO BE OVER!
NEXT, OUR TWO CHARMING MODELS EGLANTINE AND ZIZOO ARE WEARING A CREATION BY DIANE VON FURSTENBARK: 'GASLIGHT', GORGEOUS RED SATIN OUTFIT EMBELLISHED WITH SILK POMPOMS ...
THAT COLOUR WOULD GO WONDERFULLY WELL WITH YOUR COAT ... DON'T YOU THINK SO, SWEETIE?
SPRRRT!
623.B.
Roba

Follow the Lead

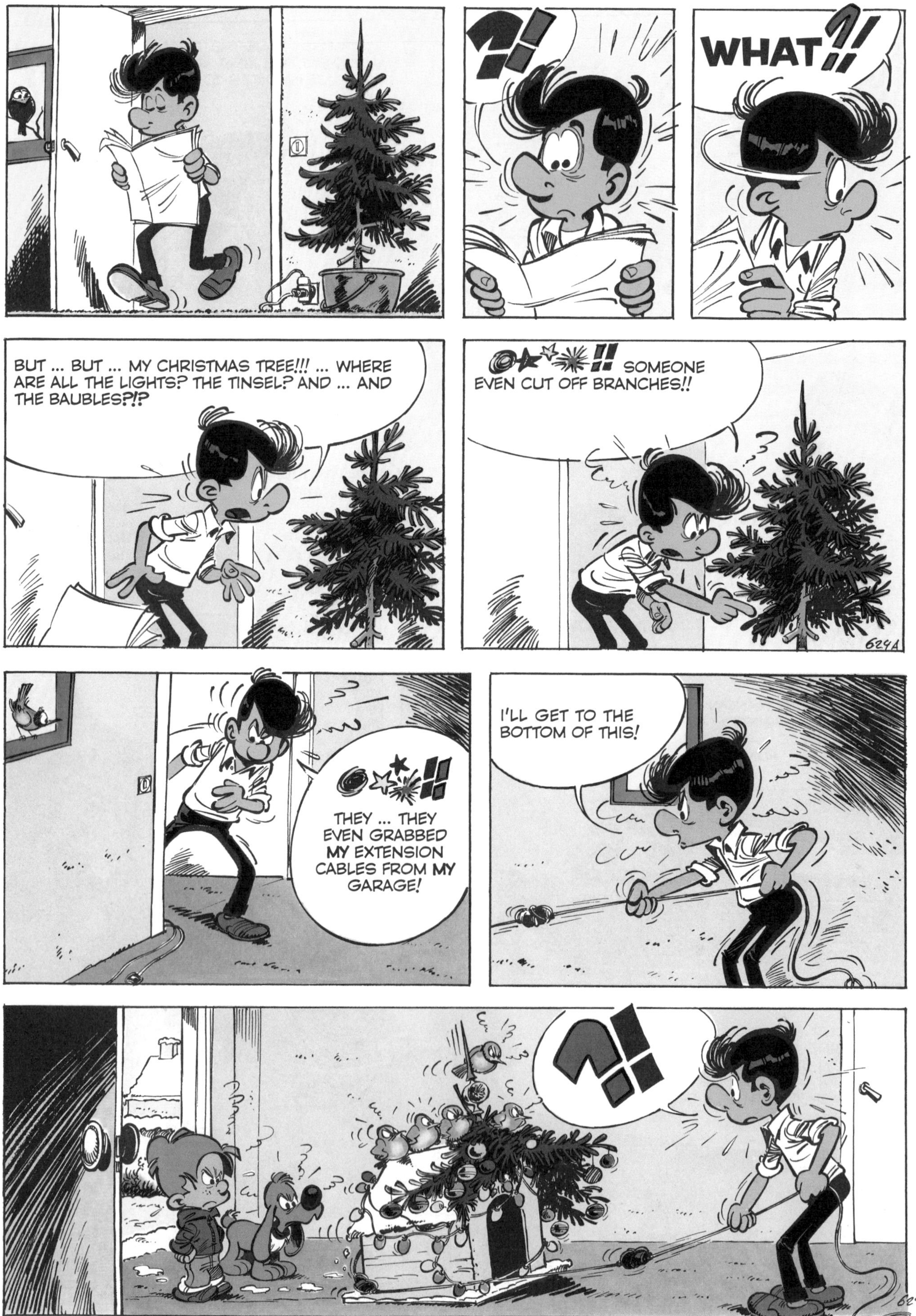

?!
WHAT?!!
BUT ... BUT ... MY CHRISTMAS TREE!!! ... WHERE ARE ALL THE LIGHTS? THE TINSEL? AND ... AND THE BAUBLES?!?
!! SOMEONE EVEN CUT OFF BRANCHES!!
THEY ... THEY EVEN GRABBED MY EXTENSION CABLES FROM MY GARAGE!
I'LL GET TO THE BOTTOM OF THIS!
?!

Avalanche

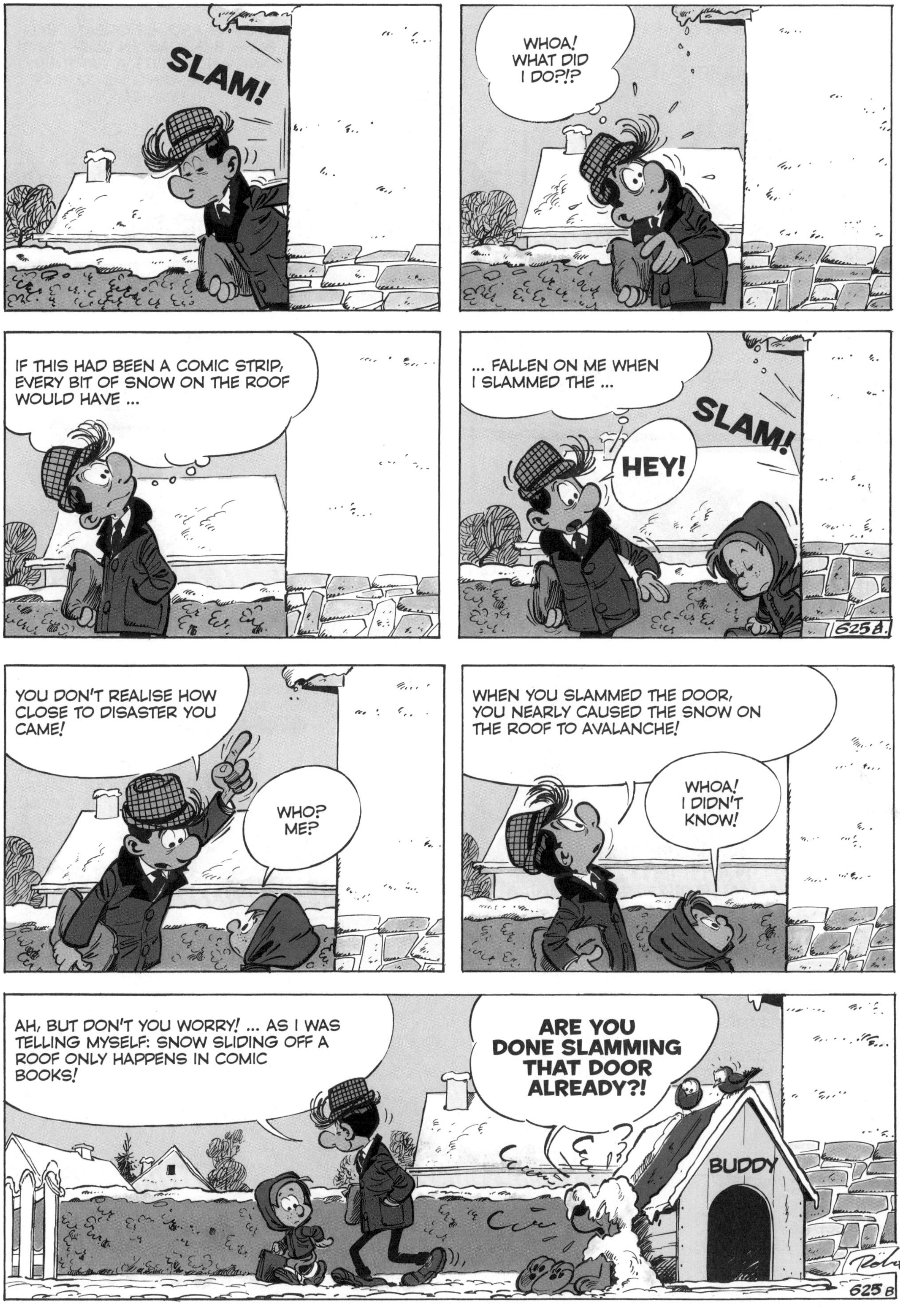
SLAM!
WHOA! WHAT DID I DO?!?
IF THIS HAD BEEN A COMIC STRIP, EVERY BIT OF SNOW ON THE ROOF WOULD HAVE ...
... FALLEN ON ME WHEN I SLAMMED THE ...
SLAM!
HEY!
625 B.
YOU DON'T REALISE HOW CLOSE TO DISASTER YOU CAME!
WHO? ME?
WHEN YOU SLAMMED THE DOOR, YOU NEARLY CAUSED THE SNOW ON THE ROOF TO AVALANCHE!
WHOA! I DIDN'T KNOW!
AH, BUT DON'T YOU WORRY! ... AS I WAS TELLING MYSELF: SNOW SLIDING OFF A ROOF ONLY HAPPENS IN COMIC BOOKS!
ARE YOU DONE SLAMMING THAT DOOR ALREADY?!
BUDDY
625 B

Winter Sports

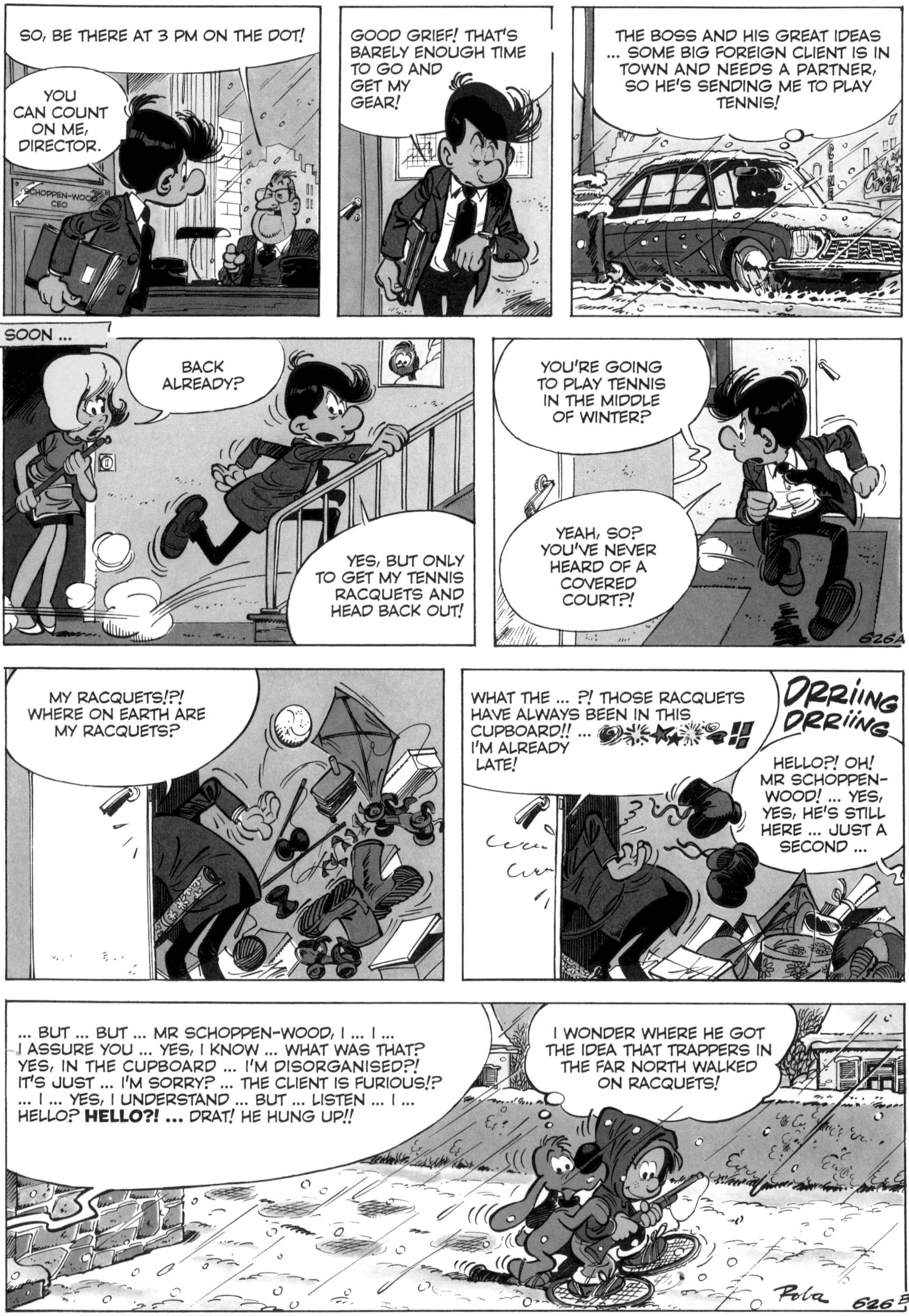
SO, BE THERE AT 3 PM ON THE DOT!
YOU CAN COUNT ON ME, DIRECTOR.
GOOD GRIEF! THAT'S BARELY ENOUGH TIME TO GO AND GET MY GEAR!
THE BOSS AND HIS GREAT IDEAS ... SOME BIG FOREIGN CLIENT IS IN TOWN AND NEEDS A PARTNER, SO HE'S SENDING ME TO PLAY TENNIS!
SOON ...
BACK ALREADY?
YES, BUT ONLY TO GET MY TENNIS RACQUETS AND HEAD BACK OUT!
YOU'RE GOING TO PLAY TENNIS IN THE MIDDLE OF WINTER?
YEAH, SO? YOU'VE NEVER HEARD OF A COVERED COURT?!
MY RACQUETS!?! WHERE ON EARTH ARE MY RACQUETS?
WHAT THE ... ?! THOSE RACQUETS HAVE ALWAYS BEEN IN THIS CUPBOARD!! ... !! I'M ALREADY LATE!
DRRIING DRRIING
HELLO?! OH! MR SCHOPPEN-WOOD! ... YES, YES, HE'S STILL HERE ... JUST A SECOND ...
... BUT ... BUT ... MR SCHOPPEN-WOOD, I ... I ... I ASSURE YOU ... YES, I KNOW ... WHAT WAS THAT? YES, IN THE CUPBOARD ... I'M DISORGANISED?! IT'S JUST ... I'M SORRY? ... THE CLIENT IS FURIOUS!? ... I ... YES, I UNDERSTAND ... BUT ... LISTEN ... I ... HELLO? **HELLO?! ...** DRAT! HE HUNG UP!!
I WONDER WHERE HE GOT THE IDEA THAT TRAPPERS IN THE FAR NORTH WALKED ON RACQUETS!

Flirting

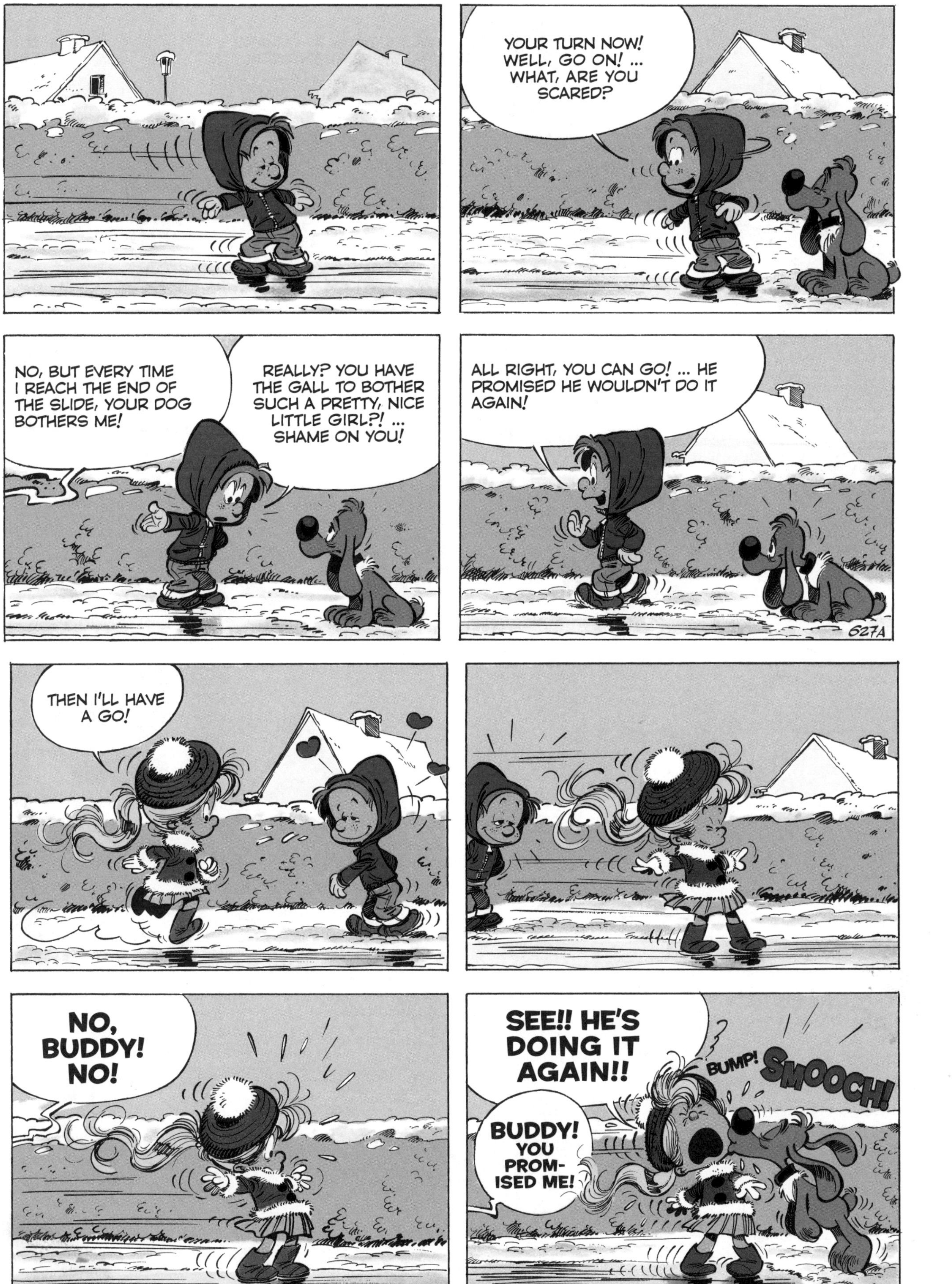
YOUR TURN NOW! WELL, GO ON! ... WHAT, ARE YOU SCARED?
NO, BUT EVERY TIME I REACH THE END OF THE SLIDE, YOUR DOG BOTHERS ME!
REALLY? YOU HAVE THE GALL TO BOTHER SUCH A PRETTY, NICE LITTLE GIRL?! ... SHAME ON YOU!
ALL RIGHT, YOU CAN GO! ... HE PROMISED HE WOULDN'T DO IT AGAIN!
627A
THEN I'LL HAVE A GO!
NO, BUDDY! NO!
SEE!! HE'S DOING IT AGAIN!!
BUMP!
SMOOCH!
BUDDY! YOU PROM-ISED ME!
Roba 627B

Billy, Buddy, and Bowling

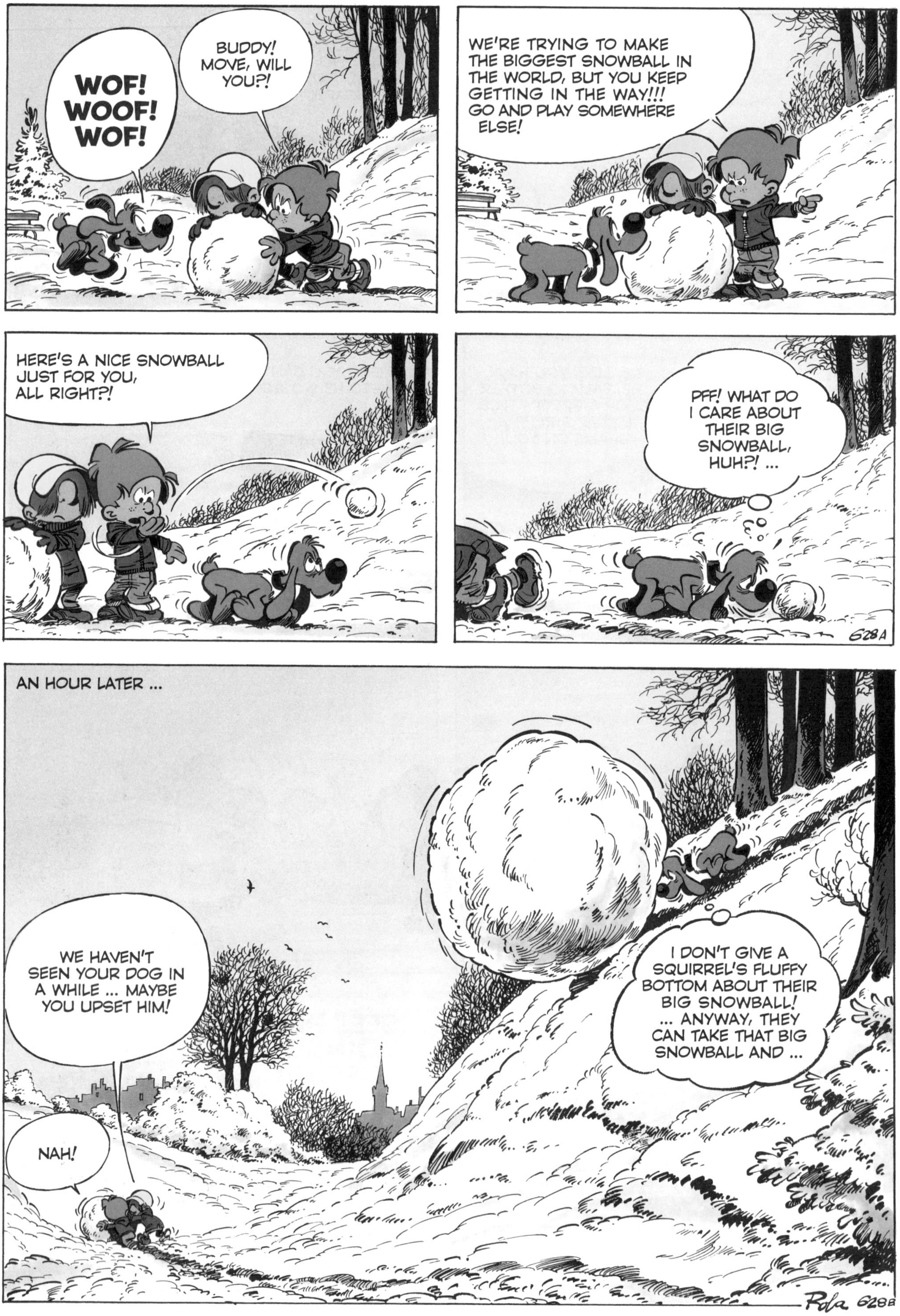

WOF! WOOF! WOF!
BUDDY! MOVE, WILL YOU?!
WE'RE TRYING TO MAKE THE BIGGEST SNOWBALL IN THE WORLD, BUT YOU KEEP GETTING IN THE WAY!!! GO AND PLAY SOMEWHERE ELSE!
HERE'S A NICE SNOWBALL JUST FOR YOU, ALL RIGHT?!
PFF! WHAT DO I CARE ABOUT THEIR BIG SNOWBALL, HUH?! ...
628A
AN HOUR LATER ...
WE HAVEN'T SEEN YOUR DOG IN A WHILE ... MAYBE YOU UPSET HIM!
NAH!
I DON'T GIVE A SQUIRREL'S FLUFFY BOTTOM ABOUT THEIR BIG SNOWBALL! ... ANYWAY, THEY CAN TAKE THAT BIG SNOWBALL AND ...
Roba 628B

Skating

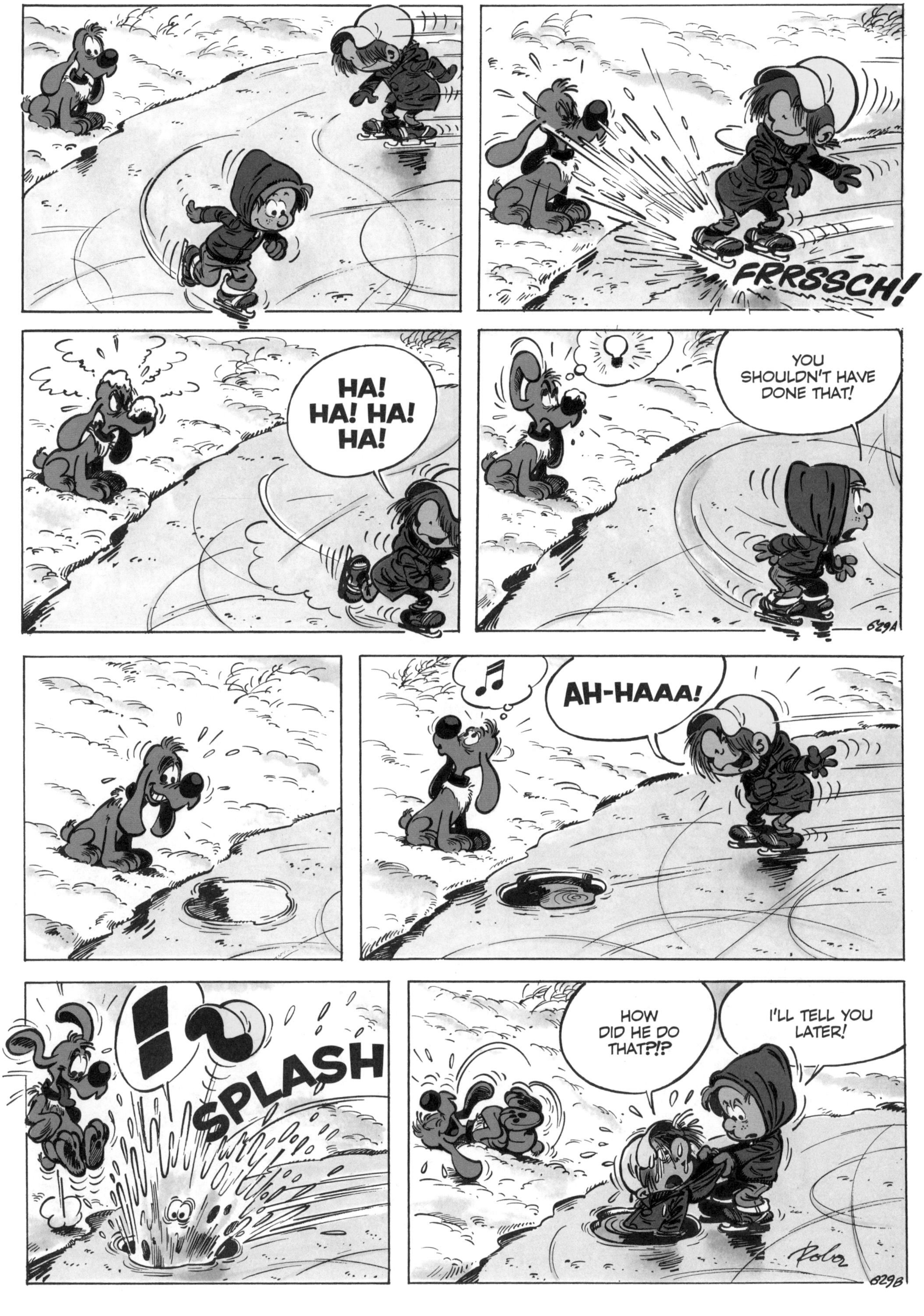
FRRSSCH!
HA! HA! HA! HA!
YOU SHOULDN'T HAVE DONE THAT!
629A
AH-HAAA!
!
SPLASH
HOW DID HE DO THAT?!?
I'LL TELL YOU LATER!
Roba
629B

Turncoat

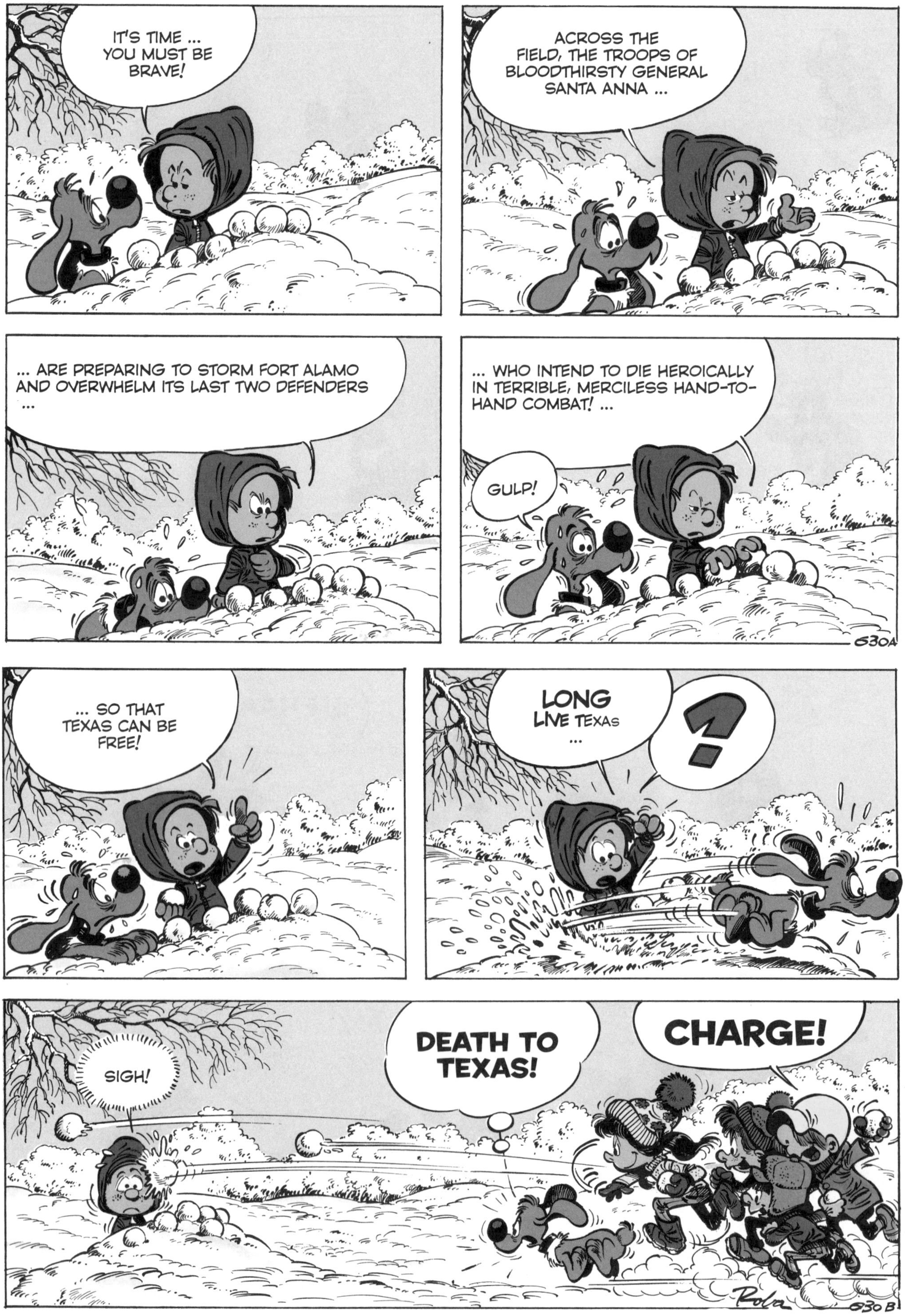
IT'S TIME ... YOU MUST BE BRAVE!
ACROSS THE FIELD, THE TROOPS OF BLOODTHIRSTY GENERAL SANTA ANNA ...
... ARE PREPARING TO STORM FORT ALAMO AND OVERWHELM ITS LAST TWO DEFENDERS ...
... WHO INTEND TO DIE HEROICALLY IN TERRIBLE, MERCILESS HAND-TO-HAND COMBAT! ...
GULP!
630A
... SO THAT TEXAS CAN BE FREE!
LONG LIVE TEXAS ...
?
SIGH!
DEATH TO TEXAS!
CHARGE!
Roba
630 B

Going Down

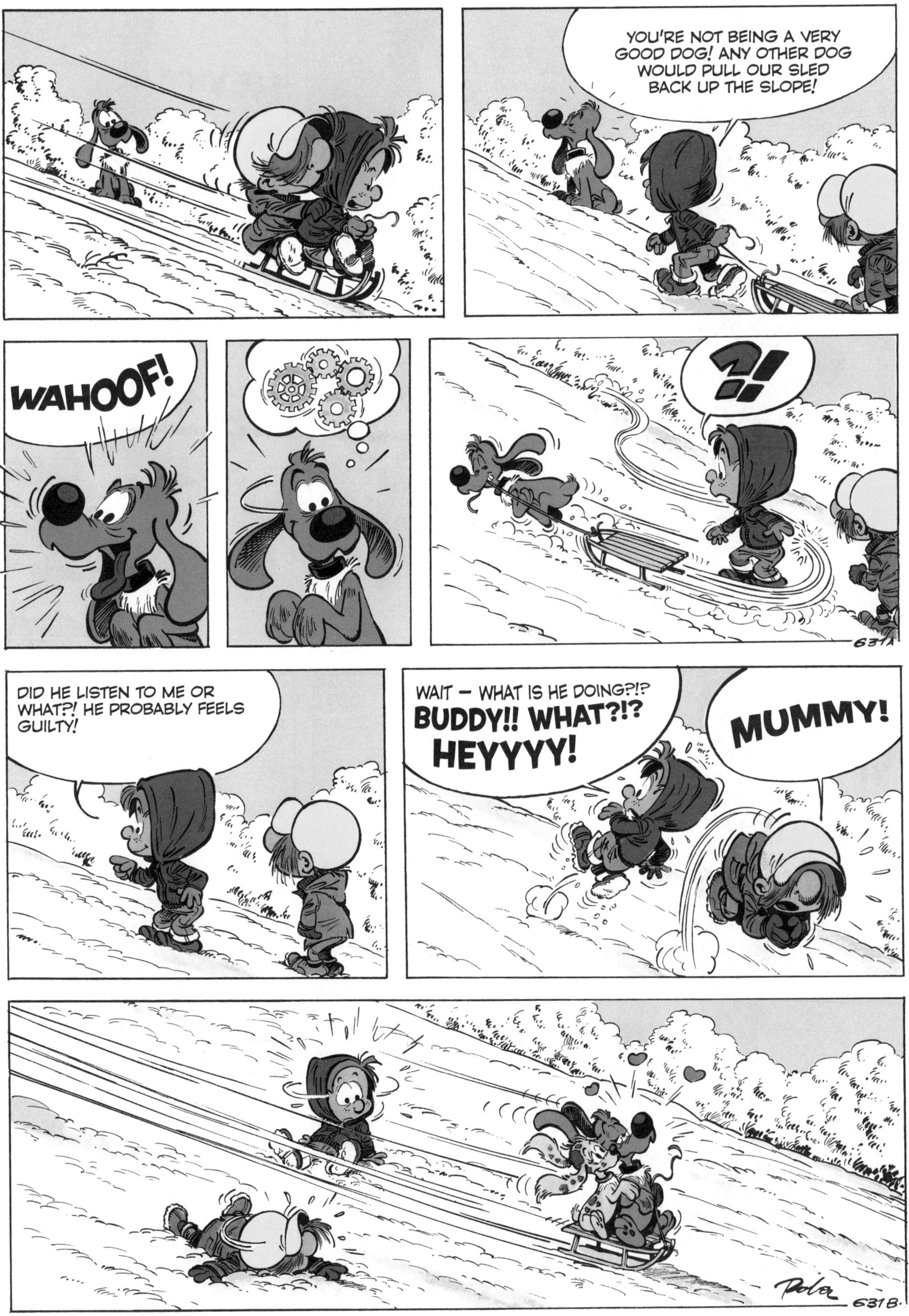
YOU'RE NOT BEING A VERY GOOD DOG! ANY OTHER DOG WOULD PULL OUR SLED BACK UP THE SLOPE!
WAHOOF!
?!
DID HE LISTEN TO ME OR WHAT?! HE PROBABLY FEELS GUILTY!
WAIT – WHAT IS HE DOING?!?
BUDDY!! WHAT?!?
HEYYYY!
MUMMY!

Nesting Box

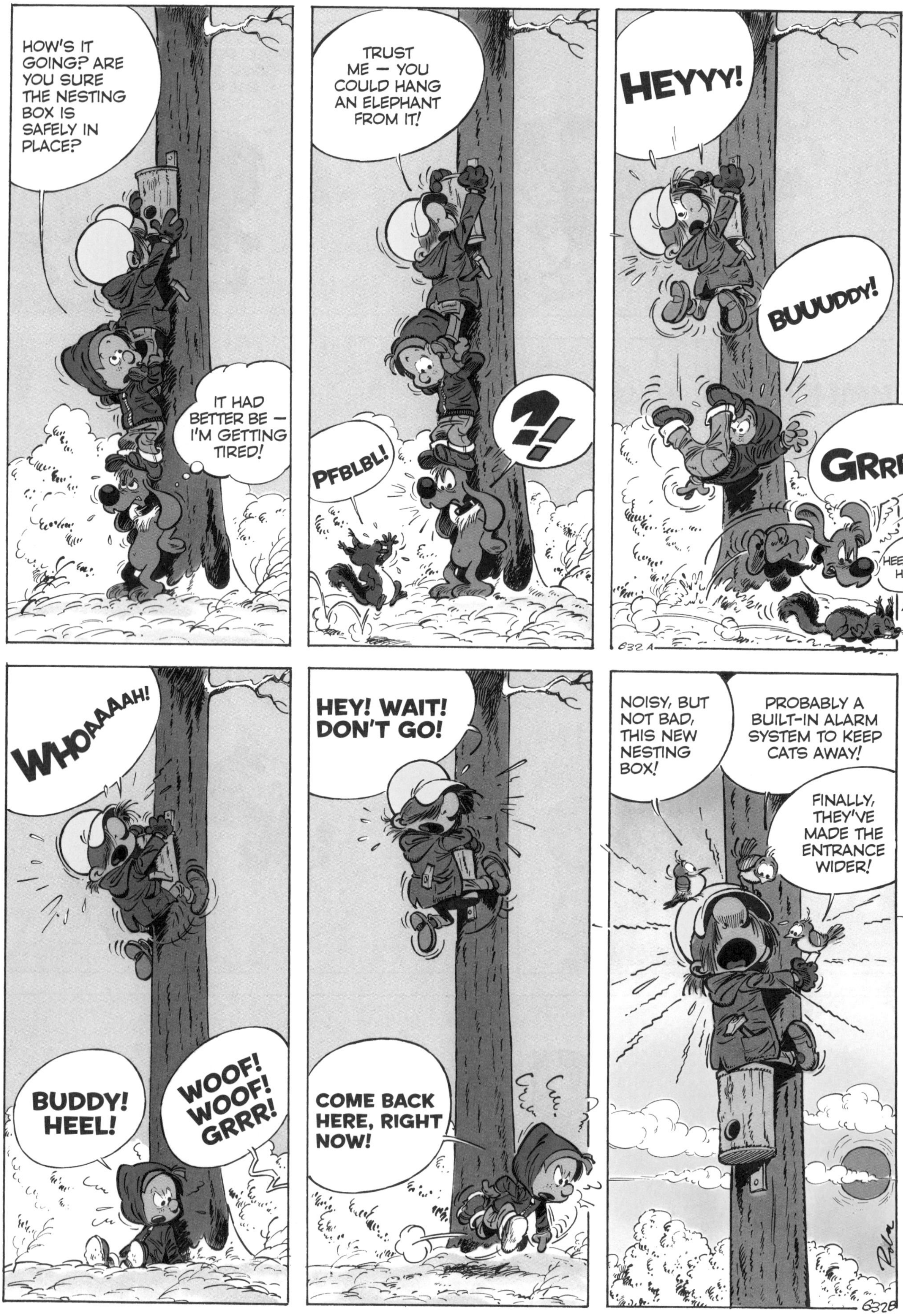

HOW'S IT GOING? ARE YOU SURE THE NESTING BOX IS SAFELY IN PLACE?
IT HAD BETTER BE — I'M GETTING TIRED!
TRUST ME — YOU COULD HANG AN ELEPHANT FROM IT!
PFBLBL!
?!
HEYYY!
BUUUDDY!
GRRR!
HEE! HEE! HEE!
632 A
WHOAAAAH!
BUDDY! HEEL!
WOOF! WOOF! GRRR!
HEY! WAIT! DON'T GO!
COME BACK HERE, RIGHT NOW!
NOISY, BUT NOT BAD, THIS NEW NESTING BOX!
PROBABLY A BUILT-IN ALARM SYSTEM TO KEEP CATS AWAY!
FINALLY, THEY'VE MADE THE ENTRANCE WIDER!
632 B

Night Watchdog

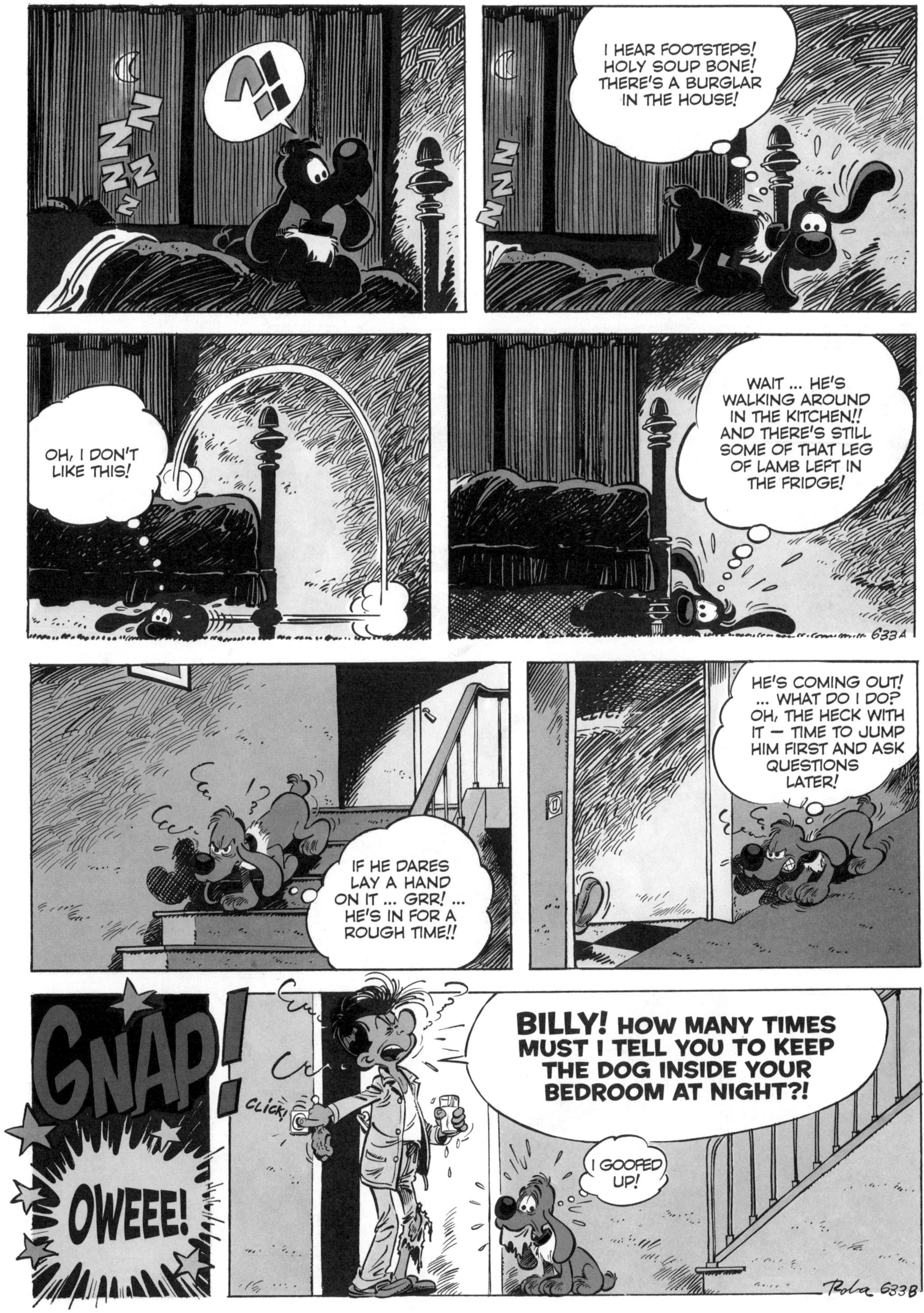

?!
I HEAR FOOTSTEPS! HOLY SOUP BONE! THERE'S A BURGLAR IN THE HOUSE!
OH, I DON'T LIKE THIS!
WAIT ... HE'S WALKING AROUND IN THE KITCHEN!! AND THERE'S STILL SOME OF THAT LEG OF LAMB LEFT IN THE FRIDGE!
IF HE DARES LAY A HAND ON IT ... GRR! ... HE'S IN FOR A ROUGH TIME!!
HE'S COMING OUT! ... WHAT DO I DO? OH, THE HECK WITH IT — TIME TO JUMP HIM FIRST AND ASK QUESTIONS LATER!
GNAP!
OWEEE!
CLICK!
BILLY! HOW MANY TIMES MUST I TELL YOU TO KEEP THE DOG INSIDE YOUR BEDROOM AT NIGHT?!
I GOOFED UP!

Good Luck Charm

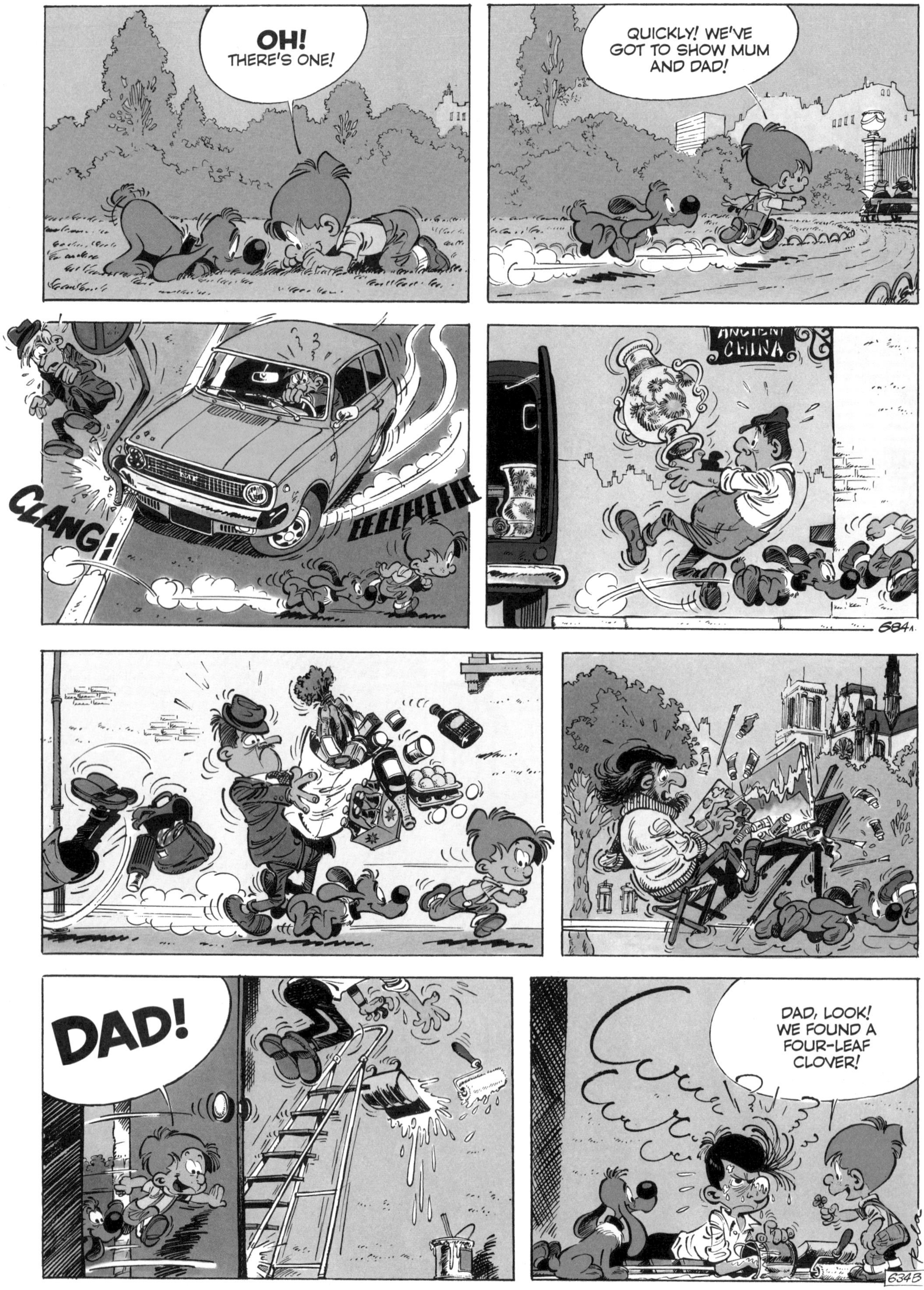
OH! THERE'S ONE!
QUICKLY! WE'VE GOT TO SHOW MUM AND DAD!
CLANG!
EEEEEEEEE
ANCIENT CHINA
DAD!
DAD, LOOK! WE FOUND A FOUR-LEAF CLOVER!

The Wrong Book

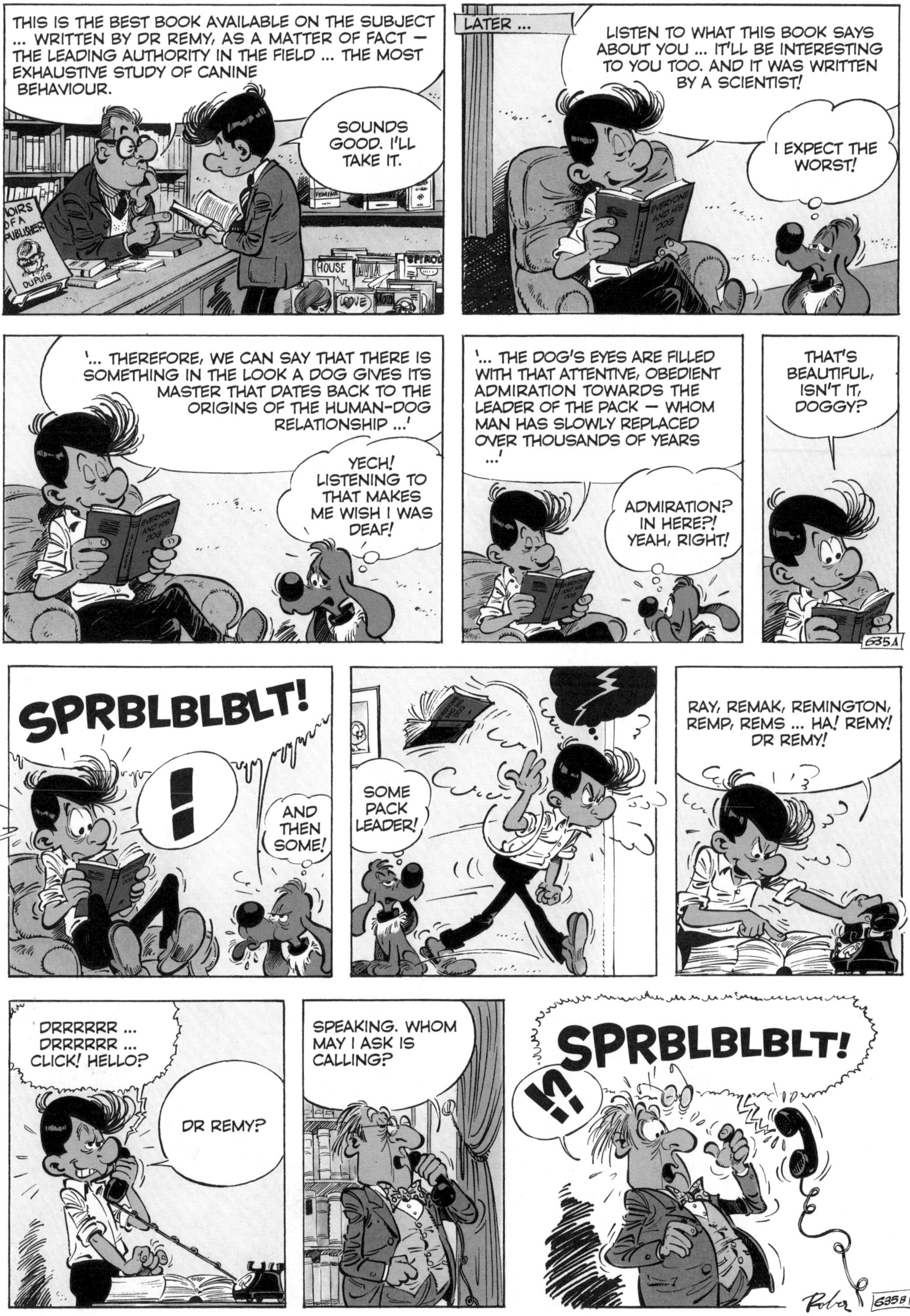
THIS IS THE BEST BOOK AVAILABLE ON THE SUBJECT ... WRITTEN BY DR REMY, AS A MATTER OF FACT — THE LEADING AUTHORITY IN THE FIELD ... THE MOST EXHAUSTIVE STUDY OF CANINE BEHAVIOUR.
SOUNDS GOOD. I'LL TAKE IT.
LATER ...
LISTEN TO WHAT THIS BOOK SAYS ABOUT YOU ... IT'LL BE INTERESTING TO YOU TOO. AND IT WAS WRITTEN BY A SCIENTIST!
I EXPECT THE WORST!
EVERYONE AND HIS DOG
'... THEREFORE, WE CAN SAY THAT THERE IS SOMETHING IN THE LOOK A DOG GIVES ITS MASTER THAT DATES BACK TO THE ORIGINS OF THE HUMAN-DOG RELATIONSHIP ...'
YECH! LISTENING TO THAT MAKES ME WISH I WAS DEAF!
'... THE DOG'S EYES ARE FILLED WITH THAT ATTENTIVE, OBEDIENT ADMIRATION TOWARDS THE LEADER OF THE PACK — WHOM MAN HAS SLOWLY REPLACED OVER THOUSANDS OF YEARS ...'
ADMIRATION? IN HERE?! YEAH, RIGHT!
THAT'S BEAUTIFUL, ISN'T IT, DOGGY?
635A
SPRBLBLBLT!
!
AND THEN SOME!
SOME PACK LEADER!
RAY, REMAK, REMINGTON, REMP, REMS ... HA! REMY! DR REMY!
DRRRRRR ... DRRRRRR ... CLICK! HELLO?
DR REMY?
SPEAKING. WHOM MAY I ASK IS CALLING?
SPRBLBLBLT!
!?
635B

Show Dog

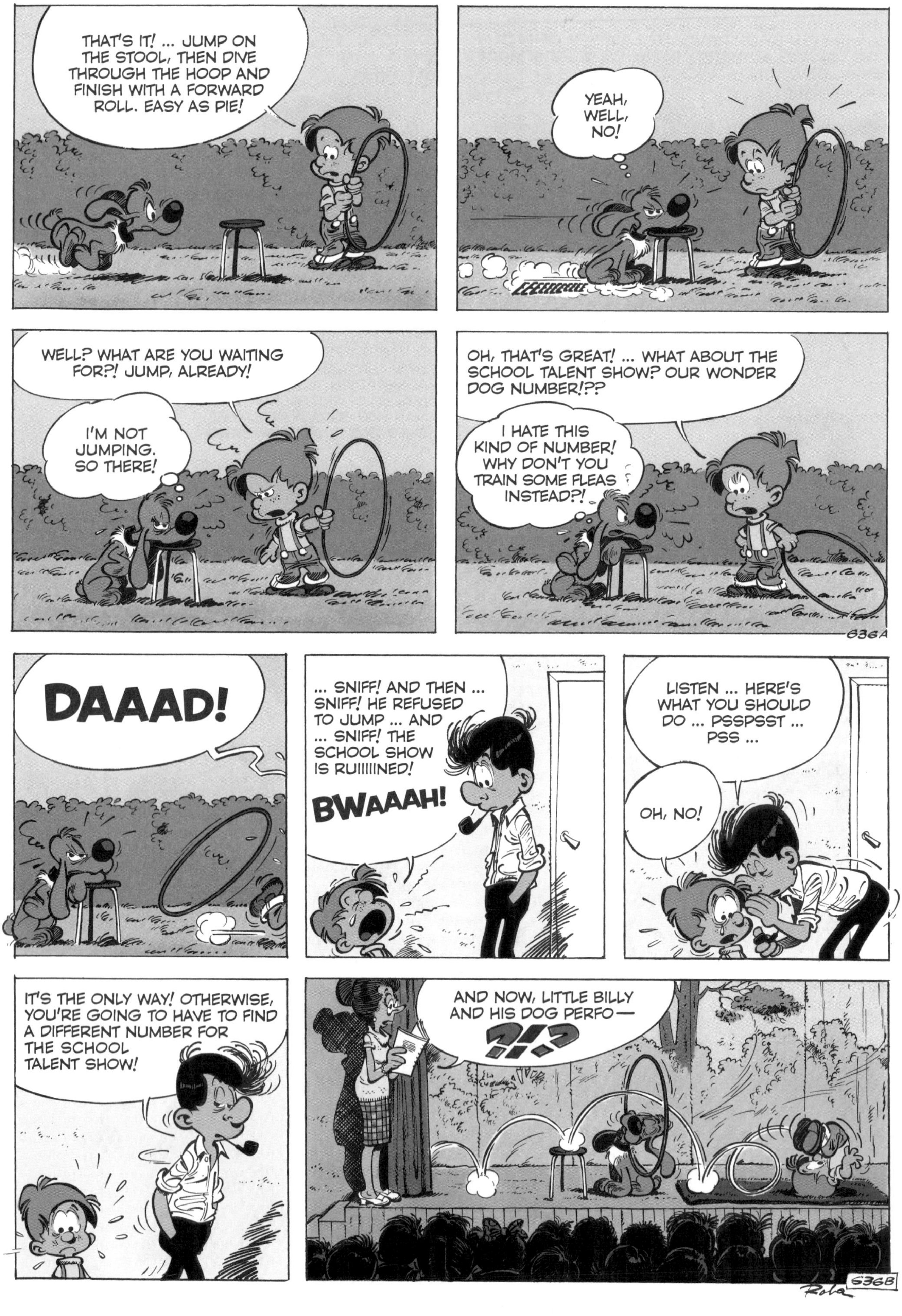
THAT'S IT! ... JUMP ON THE STOOL, THEN DIVE THROUGH THE HOOP AND FINISH WITH A FORWARD ROLL. EASY AS PIE!
YEAH, WELL, NO!
WELL? WHAT ARE YOU WAITING FOR?! JUMP, ALREADY!
I'M NOT JUMPING. SO THERE!
OH, THAT'S GREAT! ... WHAT ABOUT THE SCHOOL TALENT SHOW? OUR WONDER DOG NUMBER!??
I HATE THIS KIND OF NUMBER! WHY DON'T YOU TRAIN SOME FLEAS INSTEAD?!
636A
DAAAD!
... SNIFF! AND THEN ... SNIFF! HE REFUSED TO JUMP ... AND ... SNIFF! THE SCHOOL SHOW IS RUIIIIINED!
BWAAAH!
LISTEN ... HERE'S WHAT YOU SHOULD DO ... PSSPSST ... PSS ...
OH, NO!
IT'S THE ONLY WAY! OTHERWISE, YOU'RE GOING TO HAVE TO FIND A DIFFERENT NUMBER FOR THE SCHOOL TALENT SHOW!
AND NOW, LITTLE BILLY AND HIS DOG PERFO—
?!?
636B
Roba

Billy & Buddy

1
Billy & Buddy
REMEMBER THIS, BUDDY?
CINEBOOK

2
Billy & Buddy
BORED SILLY WITH BILLY
CINEBOOK

3
Billy & Buddy
FRIENDS FIRST
CINEBOOK

4
Billy & Buddy
IT'S A DOG'S LIFE
CINEBOOK

5
Billy & Buddy
CLOWNING AROUND
CINEBOOK

6
Billy & Buddy
BUDDY'S GANG
CINEBOOK

7
Billy & Buddy
BEWARE OF (FUNNY) DOG!
CINEBOOK

9th CINEBOOK
The 9th Art Publisher
www.cinebook.com

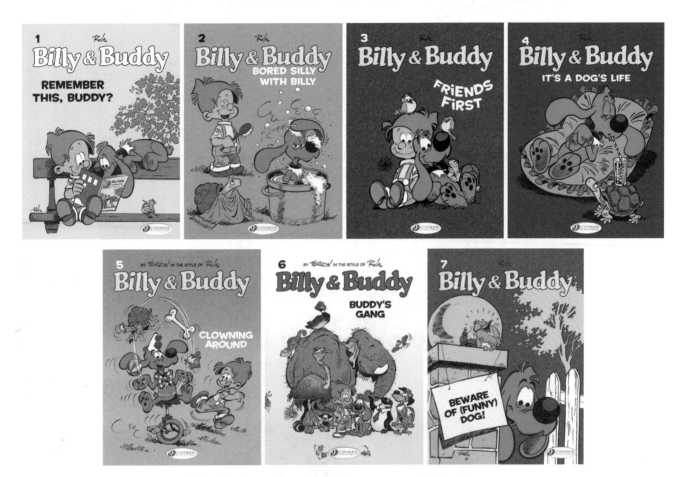

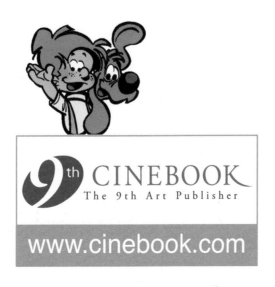

Billy & Buddy

COMING SOON

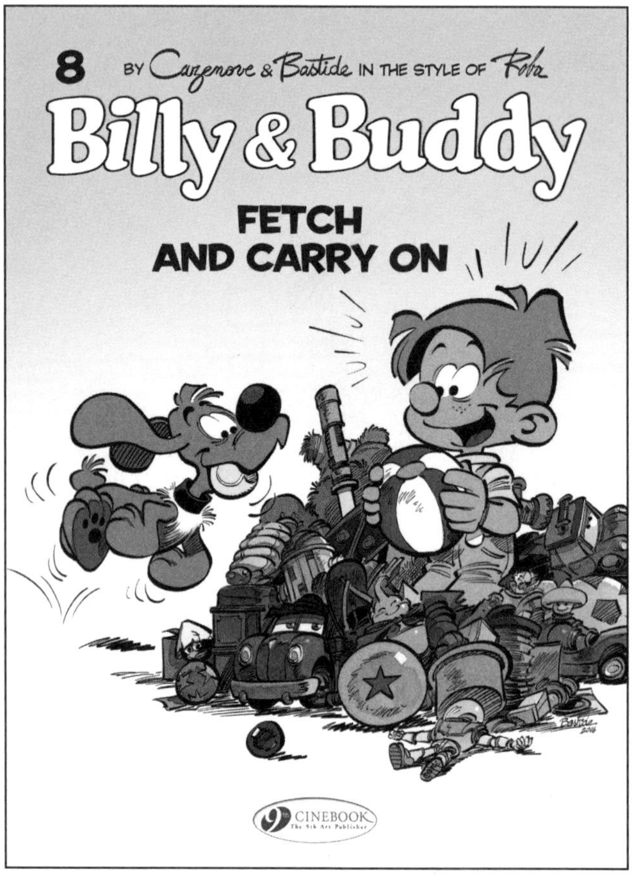
8
BY Cazenove & Bastide IN THE STYLE OF Roba
Billy & Buddy
FETCH
AND CARRY ON
CINEBOOK
The 9th Art Publisher